It Had To Happen

KIERRA ALEXIS CARTER

IT HAD TO HAPPEN

ISBN: 9781070246475

DEDICATION

Without God, I am truly nothing. I thank Him for every big and small accomplishment in my life thus far. I would like to dedicate this book to each and every person who contributed to the person I am today, especially my family and friends who love me unconditionally and never "switched up." I have also had strangers bless me in ways that left me speechless. Throughout my life, I will always think about my late grandparents, whom I loved dearly. I know that they are truly covering me with God's instruction. I want to encourage people to share their testimonies, even if they may seem embarrassing because you may never know how it will bless others. Keep in mind that *IT HAD TO HAPPEN*!!!

Photographers: Cecil Williams (Front Cover) and Tyrus Riley Sr. (Back Cover)
Publisher: DeAngela Haynes
Graphic Designer: Werly Hyppolite
Editor: Tempestt S. Johnson

IT HAD TO HAPPEN

THE PROCESS

"Sometimes things in life happen FOR us and not TO us."

INTRODUCTION

Hey guys! God gave me the vision to write this book in alignment with the motivational speaking that I do. I was praying for a title to name this book at two o'clock in the morning, and the next day around noon, I heard a commercial on the radio advertising an Easter egg hunt entitled, "It Had to Happen." Now, why was this the theme for an EASTER EGG HUNT, you may ask? I cannot answer your question because it sounds more like a revival theme or even a series my pastor may have covered a while ago. However, if this is your church, thank you because it is now the title of my book and it has really blessed me.

I never imagined publishing a book even after I was told my entire life that I should because of my experiences. I am not sure if that is a good or bad thing, but *crazy* good and bad things have happened to me in my short twenty-three years on this earth. I also understand the pain of others when they say they did not ask to be here. I used to say I would rather be a ladybug or puppy or something snazzy, but it had to happen THIS way. God's purpose will forever trump our plan.

I learned that age does not always make you wise because everyone experiences "life" at different ages. I also understand that people may not care about your life until you "make it". Well, I may not be famous or anything, but my picture is on God's refrigerator. That alone is a reminder of how I "made it" in life. Initially, I wanted to write a poetry book, but I realize it is not about me. It is about you. I am a firm believer in speaking life into others. If you follow me on social media, you may see that I literally post some form of inspiration on my stories daily. It may be me screaming at you telling you to have a good day, a quote, or my daily devotion. The crazy thing is that I do not do it for me. I share what I experience in life as an attempt to bless others, and every now and again, my followers will hit me with the "Yasss bihhhh. I needed that" or "This really blessed me."

Two completely different audiences, as you can tell, but I do not care who I am reaching. Ultimately, I look at it as Kingdom building. This book will focus on some of my personal testimonies in an attempt to provide inspirational and spiritual food for your life. I really love food. Anywho, I cannot stand books with lengthy introductions, and half of the time I skip them when I read other books (go ahead and judge me). But, I just wanted to give you the purpose of why I wrote this book.

I have come to the conclusion that I was placed on Earth to be a living sacrifice. I have the strength to constantly pour into others because God pours into me daily. My life is not my own, and I am a firm believer of being relatable, honest, and transparent. I will discuss some more of this later. I would like to close my introduction in prayer:

> ***"Father God, thank You for entrusting me with this vision to reach Your people through my testimony and encouragement. Thank You for giving me the confidence and boldness to share my story in spite of what others may***

think. Lord, use our written words to change lives, to mend broken hearts, to strengthen and inspire others to find their passion and purpose on this earth, and, most importantly, to uplift Your Kingdom. Father God, allow every person who touches this book to be set free, healed, and delivered from anything that may have them bound. In the matchless name of Jesus, I pray. Amen."

THE SEED

***"Train up a child in the way he should go; even when he is old he will not depart from it."* Proverbs 22:6**

I am Kierra Alexis Carter from Florence, South Carolina. I was born and raised in this home in East Florence, a.k.a. "the hood". (I promise this is not a children's book with all of these pictures, but I am a visual learner…stick with me).

This home granted me some of the best and worst times of my life. I lived here throughout my childhood until my senior year of high school. This house belonged to my great-grandparents, and my mother, brothers, and I lived in it with minor renovations. My uncle lived with us sometimes too. My father didn't live with us because my parents divorced when I was two years old. I didn't have a bedroom door until high school, and my dad built it from scratch. It did not have a lock, but I was ecstatic to finally have a door:, and I even took the time to paint it myself. This house occasionally had water bugs and rats from the field next door. I am absolutely petrified of both, by the way. It was liveable but was also poorly insulated, which is why we had a kerosene heater in the kitchen and extra blankets in the winter. Even our fish froze to death one winter. During the summer, we had plug-in box fans and ceiling fans. Our air or heat would break almost every year, but we made a way. Our lights would get turned off every other month and so would our water. I remember completing my homework outside in the backyard until it got dark, or on the bus so I could have light. Sometimes, we used to boil a lot of water on the stove, and pour it in the bathtub to wash. It was a tough time when both the lights and water were off, but we made a way.

My mom was a single parent of three who always figured out how to make a way out of no way. My eldest brother is almost twelve years older than me, and he lived with our dad or on his own during my upbringing. I can say we never went hungry because we had food stamps. In fact, we paid for everything with food stamps. I even got my hair done with them. We had name brand everything! But, I also would hear gunshots almost every day, a crackhead stormed in the kitchen during dinner once, and I even witnessed one of our cars being stolen. After the theft, I remember having to walk to the doctor's office while it was pouring rain, and a car splashed me and my mom when they drove by. We were soaked. I really thought that only happened in movies. Events like this made me tired of struggling. When my mother was without a car, walking everywhere was embarrassing to me. My pride also made me loathe asking people for rides. (If you ever gave me a ride in the past, you are greatly appreciated).

I was around eleven years old when my step-father moved in. Unfortunately, a lot of physical and verbal abuse took place in this house. My step-father was a drunk and a cheater. His toxicity had a rippling effect. One day at cheer practice I had to lie about the whips and bruises on my legs because I was beaten horribly for lying about cutting myself with a razor (I was attempting to shave). There were many nights I cried because of how poor we were, and seeing my mother cry did not make it any better. My stepfather stressed my mom out beyond measure, and it caused her to take it out on us much of the time. During this period, my brother and I felt neglected. One time my mom and step-father told us to get ready because we were heading to the beach. Being that we were children who were filled with excitement, we got ready really quickly. My brother and I, then, sat in our rooms, waiting to be called. The next thing we heard was the car cranking up: they'd left us and did not come back until the next day.

This very event, along with some others, prevented me from getting excited prematurely about anything. I do not get excited about opportunities until I am actually experiencing them. I do not even get excited when I am in route to vacation because I feel like anything could prevent us from making it there. It may be some form of trust issues, but I am working on this soul-tie from my childhood because I realize from where it stemmed.

IT HAD TO HAPPEN

I hated being too embarrassed to invite friends over. There was even a time when both of my parents got laid off at the same time, and our lives changed forever. I was no longer spoiled with what we could afford. I can say I am an animal lover today because my pets were literally my best friends. Sounds sad, I know, but when my puppy got ran over my mom had to come to my school because I was THROUGH. We had cats, dogs, and fish (RIP to all of them). I vented to them, and they literally licked my tears off my face and cuddled with me. Affection was not big in my household at all. There were no hugs, kisses, or "I love yous", so my pets filled this void at home. That type of affection only happened at our dad's house every other weekend. I did not find out that I was attractive until my step-mother told me at the age of thirteen that I was prettier than someone I always deemed gorgeous. Thoughts of suicide entered my mind in this home because I believed the verbal abuse I received. I lost three grandparents and a friend (all in elementary school), and I was also frustrated with living a life I had no control over. My parents were not cordial after they divorced, and they argued every single time they saw each other.

It was very stressful going to different households every other weekend because we got in trouble for leaving items or coming back too late. It still affects us to this very day, especially on holidays. **(Side Note: Do not get a divorce if you can help it. The kids do not deserve to feel like they have to pick and choose a parent for the rest of their lives. It is unfair to them.)**

Now, I did have some good times in this house. I used to sneak my first love in there all the time (sorry, Mom), I had a surprise birthday party in the backyard, and I celebrated some of the best holidays in this house. My favorite memory was allowing my brother to talk me into licking a pole during the winter. My tongue got stuck, of course. The bus pulled up on my right, and my mom had a belt in her hand on the left. I snatched my tongue off so quickly and hauled my little tail straight to that bus. My tongue was sore for a week. He also put me on top of the 10-foot high storage building to get his ball and made me freefall because our mom's car pulled into the yard. Luckily, I didn't break anything, but my mom broke his behind.

Now, I was not an angel growing up. I was a smart aleck who literally said whatever was on my mind. I was four years old when I told the doctor that his breath stank. In my defense, he did have onions for lunch. I got written up the most for talking, but I had so much to say. If I thought it, I HAD to say it. I was also a tomboy. We used to explore the woods, eat sour weeds, fight each other, and chase chickens at my dad's house. Even though I played with the boys, I loved being under my first cousins. They are like the sisters I never had, and I always looked up to them. I also used to help my grandfather sell produce on the side of the road or at the flea market. One time my grandfather gave me an egg, and I took it back to my mom's house to hatch, but my dog ate it. My brothers broke the news to me empathetically. Imagine how having a pet chicken in the hood would have turned out. At the very end of the day, I do not like talking about my childhood because I am still healing from it. Most people are too yet do not realize it.

Other than my pets, my faith was also something I held on to as a child. My outlet was going to church. I have my God-fearing father to thank for that. We lived right down the street from the church, and I did not mind walking there. My mom made sure we were very active in the church, but she didn't have to force it. I thoroughly enjoyed being there, and my favorite part was singing. I had my first solo at the age of four, and after every rehearsal they asked me to pray because my faith was strong. I believed we had the potential to sing backup for Kirk Franklin. I got saved at one of his concerts at the age of eleven, and it seemed like confirmation that God had major plans for my life. I always imagined that I had the potential to become famous, as a child, but I knew that it was impossible without God. My salvation also signified what I knew could happen in my family: I would be the person to break many generational curses.

I was always known for praying. My dad prayed with us every time we had to head back to our mother's house. He made us take turns. He also randomly selected us to say grace and to pray for "traveling mercies" when we went on trips near and far. Prayer and church has always been the seed in my life. Now, I cannot say I enjoyed having church in the living room, after assuming my dad forgot that it was Sunday. Man, we used to have a whole church service in the dining room. I mean we'd have a scripture, a song, and a bible lesson. There was no "chilling" on Sundays. God, church, and prayer were instilled in me at an early age, and it means even more to me today.

I wanted to give you a little synopsis of my upbringing because each and every one of these events had to happen. As much as I wish some of these things did not occur, I understand that they had to. If it had not been for my humble upbringing, I would not be the "go-getter" I am today. In middle school, I started babysitting my church members' children. If I was broke, I would call them and ask if they needed me to watch their kids. This was my hustle almost every weekend. One time I had eight children in one setting from the ages of seven months to eleven. I racked up that night. I do not know where my church members went, but the *communion* turn up had to be something serious!

In high school, I started flipping my mother's food stamps in addition to babysitting. My mom and I would go to the store and buy assorted candy and juices in bulk. I would sell them right out of my book bag. Yep, that's right! I was a snack dealer. I did this to fundraise for the annual show choir field trip. My friends even respected me enough to sell for me without compensation. I was able to experience New York, Atlanta, Alabama, and New Orleans for the first time ever. As soon as I was of age to work, I applied for jobs on my birthday and got a call back on the same day. My first job was at a yogurt shop, and my uniform was my favorite colors: Pink and Green.

IT HAD TO HAPPEN

I have not been unemployed since the age of sixteen. I promised myself a long time ago that my children will never have to experience the struggle. If it was not for the lack of affection, I would not be the most affectionate person you'd ever meet. The way I care for my mentees, friends, family, and strangers is indescribable. I have a true passion for helping people. I knew what it was like not having anyone to talk to about your problems, and in sixth grade, I knew I wanted to become a counselor. I was wiser than my friends because I experienced the turmoil of life rather early. I started my own counseling business in sixth grade because everyone would come to me for advice anyway, so why not charge? I think it was only twenty-five cents per counseling session, but when my teacher saw me racking up, he closed my business down. That was okay, though, because we took it straight outside.

I help myself when I help people. I turned out to be a social butterfly. I am a hugger, kisser (if your face is clean…just kidding), and a verbal "expresser" of my love for people. I was a part of the chorus, dance, cheer, and step teams from elementary school through high school. I was always a natural-born-leader and choreographer. My parents did not have to force school on me either. School was something I took seriously since I started. They never really had to hound me about it. It did not make sense to be the opposite of what my circumstances said I should have been, but my pastor told me when it does not make sense, it makes faith.

My parents did not support me for wanting to become a counselor. Black parents only want their kids to become three things: (1) a doctor/nurse; (2) a lawyer; or (3) whatever they are. My parents only wanted the best for me as a first-generation college student; however, I knew what my passion was. **(Side Note: If you have a burning desire to be something and no one is cheering you on, realize that "Sometimes you have to be your own mascot." -J. Cole)**

If it were not for my step-father and my parents divorcing, I would not be as selective with men as I am now. I would not know how to value love, marriage, and the other parties affected by a toxic relationship. If it were not for my first breakup after 3 ½ years, I would not know my worth and value. I also would not have realized that the length of time you spend dating someone, does NOT exempt you from leaving them when the relationship is toxic. I would not have understood the severity of a soul tie, and how you can really pick up good and bad characteristics from a person you are connected to.

I also would not have learned to always keep a piece of myself to myself. After we broke up, I had no idea who I was because I gave him all of me. Luckily, I did not have daddy issues, so I had a man of God to mimic who was not perfect but was able to show me the qualities I would want from my future husband. I was one tough cookie. I am pretty sure my classmates would not mind telling you that.

IT HAD TO HAPPEN

I always held on to my morals, values, and beliefs. Once again, it had to happen.

THE WATERING

"Behold, I am going to send an angel before you to guard you along the way and to bring you into the place which I have prepared."**he b**

Exodus 23:20

My senior year of high school was one of the worst years of my life. Aside from winning Homecoming Queen, it was a life-changing year for extremely negative reasons. It started off good. I had a little drama, but when I ran for Homecoming Queen, I started to realize who my real friends were. My best friend ran against me and thought I was going to trash her campaign button after I asked to wear one.

I have always been an honest competitor. She was still my friend, and, although we were going for the same title, it was not that serious to jeopardize our friendship over. . . . well, to me it wasn't. My own cousin was nominated as well, and she was bold enough to tell me not to run because I always win everything and that it was not fair. She said that I needed to give someone else a chance. (**If only haters were that bold to tell YOU why they are hating on you today, the world would be a better place.**) I still ran, and I started to take a mental note of who did not tell me congratulations. Of course my cousin and "best friend" did not. Go figure.

Little high school drama was my only concern until the day my dad came to the first cheer practice of basketball season, ordering me to leave. I was so confused and defensive because I had no idea what was going on. He waited until I got in the car to tell me that the police had taken my mother from the house earlier that day and that she would not be returning for 9 months. They'd taken her overnight before, but I had no idea why. It was right before a school trip and I had to stay the night at my pastor's home, which was the same house my boyfriend of 3 ½ years lived in, because she did not want my dad to know. It sounds exciting, but I was such a wreck that I did not pay him any attention. My first lady tried to make me feel better through shopping and food, but nothing was working.

The FBI pulled me out of class to interrogate me about the incident. My mom was afraid and wanted me to say I was there, but I told the truth because my dad did not want me to be involved. At the time, I was old enough to be sent off if I did lie. I was between a rock and a hard place because a part of me wanted to save my mom, but the other part of me had to secure my own future. Contrary to my reaction to her first arrest, when my father first broke the news to me this time I was absolutely numb. I even scared my dad because I literally had ZERO emotion. I think I just said "okay." Then, we met with my pastor immediately to get the keys to her car, and I scared him with my lack of emotion as well, especially since he had witnessed my reaction to the first arrest.

I was registering what was happening and a part of me was in disbelief. I would go to the house and get clothes for a couple of days at a time and go live with my father. A week later, after not hearing from her, one of her friends in the county jail was able to schedule a visit. I missed class to go visit her, and I could not believe what I saw. The woman who gave birth to me was behind bars in a jail jumpsuit, as if she were a criminal. It was awkward at first because I did not comprehend the severity of the situation. I was given instructions to close accounts, to pay bills, and to secure our house, among other things. That day I was forced to grow up. I held my composure because I was overwhelmed with all of the things I had to do on her behalf. I had a long walk back to the car, and that is when the tears began to stream down my face. I got in the car and finally broke down. I had to hurry back to school for my next class, and I acted as if nothing had happened.

That afternoon, I told my best friend my mom got locked up, and she laughed. I lashed out at her and told her that if it were her mom I would never do such a thing. She then realized the severity, but I took another mental note of that. I started to discern underlying jealousy. I felt as if this was the most important year my mother could have missed because she missed both senior nights for football and basketball, prom, and my presiding over graduation. Around this time, I was an employee at a frozen yogurt shop, a member of show choir, a local theatre performer, the senior class president, a cheerleader, and a member of many different clubs, including the honor society. While doing all of this, I was also preparing for college.

This was a very pivotal point in my life, and I never felt so alone. My brothers were both living in North Carolina, and I was no longer a daddy's girl because I felt as if he did not make sacrifices for me like my mom did. My dad was deemed the cool parent for the longest until he tried to crack the whip eighteen years too late with my step-mother's influence. I would literally leave practice and close at work almost every night. I was providing food, gas, and money for myself, so you could not tell me that I wasn't grown. I felt like I knew everything, and no one could tell me any differently. As a result, I lost most of my high school "friends" that year. I was numb to my emotions and the emotions of others. I apologize for that (you know who you are). I broke down every day, especially when I missed phone calls from my mother, and I cried every single time I wrote her. Instead of showing my pain, I was the class clown and got put out of class quite often. Luckily, all of the office staff were my homies. Even the principal.

I mean, I got free coffee and all. They also knew my mother was crazy, and, even though she was away, they knew that it was not in my character to act out like that. This season was tough in my life. On my mother's trial date, I missed school to support her. My mom broke down when she saw me, and I had enough strength to tell her to "man up", and I joked and told her that she looked a hot mess. There was no need for both of us to be a wreck. I tried my hardest to be in good spirits when my heart was crushed because my mother was in handcuffs.

My mom was three feet away from me, but I was not allowed to touch her. Many community officials spoke on her behalf, and the courtroom was packed with family, friends, and church members. The judge had no mercy, and in a matter of a seconds, my mother was pushed out of the courtroom. That was the moment every single feeling of hurt, depression, sadness, and guilt (because I chose not to speak in court), attacked me all at once. I had a mental, physical, and emotional meltdown. I had to be carried to the car, and my pastor and first lady could not get a response out of me for an hour. Eventually, I bossed up and cheered at two games that night. Cheering was my outlet, and my pastor and first lady came to support me. They honestly did not skip a beat after my mother went away. They did not have to help, especially since they were my ex-boyfriend's parents, but I am beyond grateful for them. My heart was still broken, but like everything else, I pushed through.

I drove my mother's car to school every day until it was repossessed on a Friday afternoon in the student parking lot. My step-dad lied about making the payments. That may have been the second most humiliating day of my life. Everyone was talking about how my mother could not afford my car, but had no idea what the circumstances were. Some knew my circumstances and the jealousy in them just pushed them to pick and laugh at my mom. Of course, they never said anything to my face.

IT HAD TO HAPPEN

The first most humiliating moment of my senior year was me almost fighting a career counselor, we'll call her "Ms. Nosey Joe". (CALM DOWN BEFORE YOU JUDGE ME, NAH!!!) She was also my church member, and she was a really big help at first. She bought me toiletry items, snacks, and other things I needed. When she first found out about my mother, there was genuine support until she started accusing me of not eating and told the guidance counselor to check on me because I was losing weight. I may have been losing weight, but if you EVER heard of me, about me, or even dreamed about me, you would know that I am NOT missing any meals for anybody or anything. If anything, I eat more when I am stressed out. I honestly love food. I apologize for the rant, but I felt like it became too much when they called me in the office and made me take off my jacket and spread my arms to examine me. Then, Ms. Nosey Joe called me from working in the school store to watch me eat. I was pissed, but I still ate the food…it was Chinese by the way. While I was eating, I kept asking if I could finish working in the store because it was our busiest day, and the choir was fundraising for our annual dinner and show.

She would not dismiss me, and just when I thought she was genuine, she asked me what really happened to my mom after stating that she would never ask and only cared about my well-being. I was sick and tired of people asking me that out of nosiness, so I packed up my food and proceeded to walk out without answering her. She screamed at the top of her lungs, telling me to come back. I still proceeded to walk off until the other counselor begged me to go back. I walked back in the room, but she did not lower her voice and was in my face. I took one step to the left, and she got back in my face.

She also blocked the door so I could not exit again. I looked at the window, and she told me I would get written up if I tried to go out of the window. I lashed out and told her I didn't care. She threatened to call my pastor, and I took out my phone and called him for her. I was cursing on the phone with him because all I wanted was this lady to leave me alone before I boxed her. She was shocked, and I gave her permission to tell the principal and left. Next thing I know, my first lady was calling the school. She managed to calm me down. From that day on, the faculty and staff began to take it easy on me, and my church member never spoke to me again. Even as an honor student, I was still in between going straight to college and working full time because I was fed up with struggling. I loved working, especially since I was a first-generation college student who did not have a plan. I didn't even know how to apply for college.

I met with one of the guidance counselors, and she helped me. I was in the office every single day getting applications for local scholarships, and I filled out the applications while I was in class. I was determined to make my mother proud. My dad took me on a few college visits, and I was accepted into five different universities. I finally committed to a Historically Black College in South Carolina because they offered me the most money for academics. After faithfully filling out scholarship applications all year, I walked away with a total of $8,000 on awards night. I also presided over the graduation as Senior Class President in front of thousands of people.

Wilson High School Graduation

Jun 1, 2013

On Saturday, June 1, 192 members of the Wilson High School class of 2013 graduated at the Florence Civic Ce

I almost did not have a graduation party until friends of the family offered to throw me one, but that pushed my dad to actually throw me one (he is cheap like Julius from the sitcom *Everybody Hates Chris*). My mom was released the summer before I began college, and things slowly became better. Right before she got out, the neighborhood thugs had been watching the vacancy of our home, and though I checked in once a week, they cleared our home out. I have never felt so degraded and betrayed in my life. My mom worked hard for everything we did have, and all of it was gone. They even tore down the fence to get our washer and dryer over it. One day we went back to retrieve what was left, and a crackhead was in her bed. The bum even had on my brother's college t-shirt. I don't know who he was trying to flex for, but we ALL knew he did not go to college. My mom woke him up out of his sleep with a two-piece and drawer to his head. That was my second time calling 911 ever, and I was more afraid of my mom than I was of the man. She didn't even give my brother time to react.

I was praying that the police would not arrest her again because of her savagery, but they were afraid of her, too. During this time, we were living with my uncle and my mother and I shared a room while my brother occupied the couch. We all shared one bathroom, but the lights and water stayed on for the most part. Progress.

The watering had to happen because water is essential for us to live. Plants cannot grow without water, and neither can we. Sometimes we have to grow through what we go through. God saw it fit for me to endure this time because I needed it to survive. God took my mother from me because I began to loathe her. It was only through her absence that I learned to appreciate her. You honestly do not know what you have until it's gone, and, to God be the glory, it was not a permanent absence. I began to appreciate the sacrifices she always made. I even missed her cooking and the "curse outs." I know that sounds crazy, but her brokenness did not only break me, it pieced me together. I also learned that my decisions do not only affect me, but they affect the people around me just as much. I learned who was really supportive of me and who really was not. Everyone wants to claim you when you are doing well, but when you are down, they proceed to bury you, not knowing that you are actually a seed. This was essential because God has taken me some places where the fake and phony did not deserve to go.

I will never forget the people and the sorority that supported me every step of the way. They remained loyal when I was not loyal to myself. Ironically, though, I honestly had the best Christmas ever because of the people who blessed me during that tough time. I never wanted for anything other than my mother. I had a church member go out of her way to take me to school every morning; I had church members take me out to dinner every Sunday; I won a complete prom makeover; and my first lady even held me for hours during my weakest moments.

Also, a local sorority granted me a scholarship and paid for the majority of my dormitory supplies. I am now a member of that same sorority. It took a garden to help me blossom through the concrete, and I am ever so grateful for them. That year taught me independence. My roots were strong enough to withstand everything that was thrown at me, and now I can say it had to happen.

THE CONCRETE

For I know the plans I have for you," declares the Lord, "plans to prosper you and not to harm you, plans to give you hope and a future. Jeremiah 29:11

My mom, dad, and friend helped me move into my dormitory. I was excited to begin my first year of college. I didn't go wild because I honestly did whatever I wanted in high school, and my older brother had already introduced me to certain things so they would not be new when I got to college. I partied, but school came first. And, no matter what time I got in on Saturday night, I always went to church on Sunday. I even walked alone some Sundays (it was across the street…Don't get me wrong, I'll walk for God, but I do have asthma so it will not be very far). Freshman year started off great.

I was popular after being named the chaplain of my dorm, winning the titles Miss Freshman and Miss Student Support Services, and becoming a cheerleader. However, I always remembered what my show choir teacher in high school told me. She said I was going to be in for a rude awakening when I got to college because there was always going to be someone better than me at what I did. From that day on, I strived to be the best in everything that I did.

In spite of all of the preparation, I had a very hard time adjusting. My roommate was extremely wild and loved drama. When we met before school started, I got to know her better, and I learned that she was a firecracker from New Jersey. But, I had no idea that this girl would have had drama with everyone on the hall. Seeing this behavior made me stop hanging out with her crew early on, but the deal breaker for the two of us was when she was in the middle of a party twerking on the floor. I could not get with the program. We still talked in the room, but we did not hang out on campus because I did not want to mess up my reputation.

My favorite memory of her was her twerking to a gospel song I was playing in our room. She did not know any better, but I walked in the room the next day and she was playing it…no twerking this time. That was the first gospel song she ever played around me, and I was happy she was getting some Jesus by rooming with me. My worst memory was her not telling me she burned my hair out with a curling rod in the back, and I always let her in my head because she claimed she was the best. She neglected to tell me at the time, and I found out when I went to get a sew-in. Unfortunately, I didn't find out until after she left the school, which was after the second semester. We did not make it as roommates for one semester because all of the girls on our hall wanted to fight her. I have not had a roommate since. Thank God.

I also suffered from a lot of health issues. Nothing is scarier than going to the doctor without your mom for the first time. I was diagnosed with sinusitis at home after being misdiagnosed at the local hospital. I was on antibiotics for a month, and one of the side effects was numbing of the legs. I had to take a break from cheering and had to deal with the agony of knowing that if the medicine did not work, I would have to get surgery. The surgery would have taken me out for the rest of the season, but to God be the glory, it did not, and the medicine worked.

I was also diagnosed with scoliosis, and they told me if my curve intensified, I would have to have surgery, which would have ended my ability to dance and cheer throughout my entire matriculation. Dancing and cheering had been my passion since the age of four, so I was devastated by this news. With more tests, they found that my curve was pretty permanent, and, although I have aches every now and again, I was still able to cheer. Cheering seemed safe enough until I sprained my ankle after being dropped out of a stunt. However, I still cheered on it because we were playing our rivals, and I did not want to let the team down. I endured the pain of sticking it in ice immediately afterward…what a dummy.

After my sicknesses, I *bossed up* and participated in my first pageant on campus. I won everything except the title. I vowed never to do a pageant again. I mean, my feelings were shot, but that humbled me even more. The pageant results soon became a distant memory, but the last thing I remember about my freshman year was being called in to pray for a friend who had just lost her father.

I knew I was the chaplain of my dorm and all, but I was under the impression that I would just have to pray in dorm meetings. I was not prepared for that, but I used the strength I knew I had to pray her through this tough time. I mean, I prayed heaven down, too. This is when I discovered a new kind of strength that I possessed. If it was not for me losing multiple relatives and a friend, I would not have been able to pray for her. It had to happen.

Toward the end of my freshman year, I ran for a secretary position, and I lost. My church member signed me up for a pageant back at home, and I lost that too. I was so sick of taking "Ls." In fact, I decided to chill my sophomore year. At that time, I didn't know I was receiving all of those "no's" in order to prepare me for a season of "yes". Before I knew it, I received an email stating that I was accepted into the honors college that I had worked tirelessly to get into that summer. In other words, my tuition was covered for the next three years. When it seems as if the enemy is telling you no, God will flip the script and give you a BIG "YES".

My next "yes" came from attempting to participate in the local pageant back at home again. I know I declared that I was not participating in a pageant ever again, but I was not going to allow someone to represent my city who was not from there again. I went on YouTube and studied pageant poses, walks, and questions. I did not come to play this time. The first time was very rushed, and I was ignorant and injured. This time was EVEN MORE rushed, but I knew enough to look like I knew the proper pageant etiquette.

I didn't even have $100 to enter; but I asked different people, and my church member gave me the remainder. I will never forget the people who sowed into my dreams. Feeling empowered by all of the support, I performed to the best of my ability, and in the end, they did not call my name for any preliminaries. I was so discouraged, and my mom sensed it.

When I heard my name being called as the winner, I was SO extra. I cried like a little baby. Who knew a girl from the hood could be the first African American to represent her entire city as Miss Florence 2015. It was lit! I had literally over 30 engagements that year. I was able to give back to so many people, and I was on an ultimate high. I loved community service, and I mainly served in the community I was raised in to show the children that their upbringing does not limit them from following their dreams. My mother was my unofficial manager, and she drove me to almost every event.

SCNOW

YouTube and God lead Kierra Carter to Miss Florence crown

Kierra Carter was crowned Miss Florence 2015 o...

BY SHAMIRA McCRAY Morning News

I, then, competed in the state pageant. The pageant world is cruel behind the scenes. I have never been judged so much in one week; it was ridiculous. I wanted to fight since the first day I got there, but I knew that I had to remain classy. There were over 50 contestants, and only 5 looked like me, and, of course, they thought we all looked alike. They backstabbed each other very often.

IT HAD TO HAPPEN

I remember when we all took a bus to McDonald's and our meal was covered. Did you say a free meal? Yes, a free meal. The other "down to earth" girls and I went ham. I ordered a Big Mac meal with a tea AND a mocha frappe. Some girls ordered apples and water, and some girls refused to order anything. While they were whispering and staring at us, I was living my best life. I felt so bad for them. One night I walked in with a Bojangles' box, eating my two-piece in the dressing room, and everyone had an uproar about that. I did not care, and the last thing I was going to do for anybody was starve myself (unless I am fasting, of course).

The experience and exposure was a dream come true, but it was not worth the headache behind the scenes. I am too genuine and honest to endure that voluntarily. I was not going to tell you guys this because I wanted you to think I behaved the entire week, but there was one little thing. My pageant sister came to me very upset saying that the other teens were talking about her because she did a push up with one hand. This was toward the end of the pageant week, and I walked in a room of over 50 girls and very loudly asked if anyone had a problem with her.

No one said anything, and I said, "Oh I didn't think so," and walked out. I refused to hold my tongue any longer, and I did not like how that week made me feel at all. I didn't win the state title, but I was not upset because my main focus was representing and bringing exposure to my city. I lost friends on campus after I became Miss

Florence, but because it had been happening since high school, I just let them go. I told my dad that I felt like I kept getting the short end of the stick when it came to friendships, but he told me to consider it the blessed end.

That year, two girls told me that they did not like me because I thought I was "all that," and then they got to know me and loved me. I told them that they had a personal problem with me because THEY thought I was "all that." I knew the internal battles I was fighting, and they kept me humble. I, then, realized that I either inspired or intimidated people, but at the time I liked doing both.

I had my share of drama, too. Not all of it stemmed from jealousy either. I used to gossip, and of course, things would get back to the person. I never got into a screaming match, but there were some heated discussions. Some were and were not my fault. I made it out of college without fighting, so I think I was pretty okay.

I also had a guy I was dealing with who cheated on me more than once, and one of the girls was my teammate and mentee. The betrayal was real. This guy even made me a candlelit dinner in an attempt to apologize, and my mentee posted a picture with his dog the very next day. So stupid. He later referred to me as a female dog, and that was the last straw. I promise.

When I ran for Miss Homecoming, I lost. I felt discouraged because it was a huge position. My speech was trash, though, because I was nervous. People even laughed in my face afterwards. There were a lot of phony things taking place during that time. Some people even said I was getting too "crown happy" and that I deserved to lose, but I knew what I was preparing myself for.

I wanted to be the university queen my senior year, so my strategy was to have my name recognized. The university queen was my mentor, during my freshman year, and I wanted to follow in her footsteps. It seemed as if this was starting to be the season of "no" again, but God was setting me up for another "yes". My grand-aunt (my last grandparent figure), and my best friend's mother died that year. We prayed together during this tough time. After these particular deaths, I had a burning desire to reach more people during their most difficult times. After many meetings and strategic planning, God gave me the vision to start an organization on campus called Helping Everyone Avoid Loneliness (H.E.A.L).

H.E.A.L is a support group for college students who struggle with internal obstacles due to death or just everyday life. This organization saved my life as well as many others' lives. God has moved miraculously in this organization. At every interest meeting, we had people share their personal testimonies, and I shared mine to set the atmosphere. I wanted to create a nonjudgmental atmosphere, so I believed that being transparent was the only way to do that. I also implemented a game called "Circle of Truth." I would play worship music in the background, and I would tell my members to step into the circle if the statement applied to them. I started off with very simple questions, and as the game progressed, they slowly intensified. I went from asking if they liked café food to ultimately asking if they ever dealt with depression, anxiety, or low self-esteem. One boy felt led to share his testimony for the first time in an interest meeting and it really blessed others. Other people gained enough courage to share their testimonies for the first time as well because they could relate to him.

In other meetings, we had nights catered to the students. I always asked them to write down their favorite hobbies, and I responded accordingly. We had game night, movie night, art night, and even affirmation night. We also helped the elderly in the nursing home avoid loneliness by periodically doing artsy activities with them. One of my H.E.A.L. members transferred and began a chapter in North Carolina. H.E.A.L was a breeding ground for deliverance, emotional healing, and breakthrough. It was also my platform for Miss South

Carolina. It had to happen. I was stronger emotionally than ever before that year.

My junior year was tough. I was going out for a sorority and the process was suddenly canceled. I remember I was asleep when I received a call informing me that the intake process was canceled. My heart sank to the floor because I had been longing to join this sisterhood since the age of four. Not only did they help while my mom was away, but I was also in their cotillion and summer camps. After already being hurt for not being able to proceed, someone had to start a rumor. Somehow my name was put in the bowl to be stirred up for allegedly calling nationals because I was not eligible. I honestly had absolutely no reason to do such a thing because I had all of my ducks in a row, from having a 4.0 GPA to a prestigious résumé to flawless recommendation letters from Sorors in high positions. This hurt me to the core because over eighty girls were led to believe that I was the reason for their dreams being declined.

I mean the rumor got out to other schools, and I was receiving calls from the east, west, north and south. I was officially humiliated. Students who once spoke to me stopped, and I would get stares every time I entered a building. Even some boys on campus had beef with me. Out of all of the students who accused me, only three were real enough to ask me if it was true or not. Apparently, a letter of lies was written about me being hazed and given to the advisor. I promise I did not take anyone's man, guys. The girl who wrote it lost a race to me, she did not make the cheer squad, and a guy she liked was interested in me. So, I understand her jealousy, but she went too far when she called me trying to be messy.

I hung up in her face because she was on speaker phone and was trying to get a reaction out of me. During this process, security and two sorority girls busted into my room to investigate me on two separate occasions. I was also called out of class to speak with the first lady of the WHOLE University about this issue, and I had to speak to the advisor of the sorority, too. The advisor had no reports of anyone calling nationals, but because the process was canceled, she could not contact the candidates to tell them that the allegations against me were false. People I went to high school with even started rumors about me being "blackballed" from the entire organization. My anxiety levels were never so high until that year. I went home almost every weekend.

I had my two best friends from high school pick me up to stay with them because they were only 40 minutes away. (They are literally still my besties and travel buddies to this very day.) While at school, I could not even rest well because I feared that someone would bang on my door requesting me to meet with someone else concerning this issue. Oh, and the Vice President of the university almost would not allow me to run for my dream title because of this lie. This lie ruined my self-esteem and confidence. I cried and prayed daily for the truth to be revealed. The worst part was not being lied on or talked about OR investigated. The worst part was that I was actually being labeled as a selfish person. They said that I said, "If I can't get it, nobody can."

If there ever came a day where my involvement would jeopardize 1-80 other people, I would drop it. I have always been known as an altruistic person, and for my character to be portrayed as crass killed me inside. The lies continued when someone told the first lady of the university that they saw me smoking weed on the side of the road. The first lady called me to see if it was true, but I was in Alabama for a cheer competition, so that was clearly a lie. That was right before I went on the floor to compete, too -- talk about a major distraction. But, once again I had to suck it up and be there for the squad.

I went through a season of depression, which killed my passion for many other things. I was falling out of love with cheering, and before I knew it, I fell out with half of the squad and the coach. Once again, just like in high school, I felt like I had my own back, and I shut others out and was disloyal to them (I apologize, Cheer Pals).

When I called my father to vent about it, he said that there was a pattern with me falling out with girls and that the common denominator was me. Those words were so hurtful because I was quick to put jealousy on other people instead of reflecting on my own flaws. That was the only other time I felt as if the world would have been better without me. I also was talking to some knucklehead who made me an option and his video games a priority during one of the most difficult times of my life. For some reason, I kept settling for knuckleheads. Lawd, the deception from the enemy was real on that day.

My own coach did not have my back because she saw how cheering was no longer a priority, and she found out that I wanted to join a different sorority from hers. She turned on me the most. However, I DID tell her that no one enjoyed cheering anymore because of her (I thought she would appreciate the honesty, but boy was I wrong). I mean, she asked if it was her fault, and I said "yes." However, I was not just speaking for myself. That day her exact words were, "Running for that title is going to run you into the ground." Her words stung. I have been through a lot, but that was the first time in my life that someone implied that I could not accomplish something. Those words hardened my heart, and I had to prove her wrong. I was co-captain of the squad and had been cheering for 16 years around that time. I had to try out again, but I was not going to because I knew that I was running to be the queen of the university and did not want to do both.

I did not want to end up regretting it, so I came up with a dance and cheer the night before. When it was time to give the results on who made the squad, my coach lied to the squad and told them that I did not care about them and that I was self-centered. I stood before her in my tryout and told her that I would humble myself and not allow my personal issues to transfer onto the squad. I expressed how apologetic I was, but she kept criticizing and lying on me. I remained quiet when everything in me wanted to stop her. She even voiced that my performance was not good enough for her, and I know I gave it my all: I auditioned with just as much energy as I had given the last three years. From that point, I knew her mind was already made up before I even tried out. She eventually announced in front of the squad that she could not take me back.

Everyone was shocked because at the end of the day I contributed a lot to the team, but I was too flawed in her eyes. I called my dad immediately afterward, and I did not shed one tear. I was not upset with the results because I started not to try out anyway. I also knew that greater opportunities were coming because she only made me hungrier for that title. Nevertheless, I was upset about being lied on.

Being falsely accused of being selfish for the second time hurt me. However, I was able to plead my case to the squad, and they already knew how extra the coach could be, so it was not that bad. The closer we got to campaign season, the more I was punking out on running for my dream title because I felt like the rumor ruined my chances of getting the student votes. That night was when I vowed to change my attitude about my situation.

I declared that I was no longer going to tell God how big my storm was, but I was going to tell the storm how big my God is. I was sick of excuses, depression, and defeat. I finally had peace within myself that allowed me to hang out on campus, to sit with people I did not know in the café, and to speak to everyone I crossed paths with just as I had done before.

Campaign season started, and I gave it everything I had. It was a tiring week campaigning and preparing for a pageant, but I was not stressed because I had prepared four months in advance. I did not go broke trying to win either. Genuinely talking to people and caring about what they cared about got me ahead. This was the biggest race for the title that my university has ever had, and during pageant rehearsals, I would get discouraged because most of the girls were so intimidated by me. The director even had to scold them for cheering each other on, but when it came to me, you could hear a cricket Crip-walking on a cotton ball.

The main thing that made me want to quit was seeing my former pageant director call one of the other contestants. This girl went on my social media to reach out to my pageant director and personal trainer for this pageant, AND they helped her. I mean, I probably would have done it for a coin too, but at the time I felt betrayed. To add to that betrayal, my cheer coach had her god-children helping the same girl out with her talent. My former coach planned pageant ideas with my former teammate. The same teammate made my coach keep us after cheer practice because she felt as if I was plotting against her for this pageant every time I saw her. I thought that was the pettiest thing. Through my hunger and exhaustion, after a three-hour cheer practice, I told my teammate that she thought she was more important in my life than she really was. I know that was rude, but I was an honest competitor. I did not have time for the foolery and that left a bad taste in my coach's mouth. So, when my coach's god-daughters walked in on the pageant rehearsal after I saw my director call, I had to act as if my heart did not sink into my underwear at that moment. Then, when the girl mentioned my pageant director's and the trainer's names on the phone, it was too much. I was losing my mind, and I could not wait to leave pageant rehearsal that night.

I called my dad immediately after practice was over to tell him what I had pieced together. His response was not what I was expecting. My dad said, "If you are worried about what she is doing, tell me so I won't come to the pageant." My dad has never talked to me like that. He proceeded to ask me if I prayed and fasted on behalf of this title, and I had an attitude because I already told him that I did. He said that while she was depending on man, I was focusing on God. He said that there was no comparison, and that I should not allow that to distract me.

After that conversation, I knew that the enemy was trying to punk me, and I was not having it. The next day, I killed all preliminaries in the pageant. I had a lot of fans, which boosted my confidence because I felt as if everyone was going to "BOO" and throw rotten tomatoes at me. Okay, not that extreme, but I felt as if people were not going to show me love. Ironically, my former cheer coach texted me,

"You're doing great, boo," during the pageant and sat on the front row. I did not say thank you until the next day.

The pageant went by so fast, and, although there were seven other contestants, I was told it was between me and another girl. That did not make me feel any better. The day of the election results was so nerve-racking. My friend, who was running for the king title, and I left campus as soon as we heard that the email was coming (he is just as extra as I am). We pulled in an abandoned bank parking lot and prayed as gospel music played in the background.

We heard the email notification and saw that he won, and we went crazy. We then searched for my name, and my name did not appear on the email. I then found out that they were saving the queen and president results for last. Around that time, I ran to my dorm, and I was heading up the stairs when I received a text telling me to go to the queen's advisor's office. I took off running, and on the way there, someone called me and told me congratulations. I screamed like someone ate my leftovers, y'all. When I finally made it to the office, everyone was so happy for me.

My friend had to call my parents and tell them the news for me because I could not stop crying. At that moment, all I could think about was how faithful God was, and how He helped me overcome all the obstacles I faced. My former cheer coach called me twice, and I ignored her calls. I called the deacon (my dad) and asked if I was wrong for ignoring her and he said, "No, baby girl. If people can't accept you at your lowest, they do not deserve to claim you at your highest."

That was the end of that. I won the biggest race in the history of my university. I cried for a good 30 minutes. God used each and every one of those setbacks to prepare me for this major comeback. God made my enemies my footstool right in front of my very eyes. My faith was tested, but I remember that they lied and talked about Jesus, too. His strength pulled me through. It had to happen.

Unfortunately, after this, I had the worst summer ever. I was the only person still living on campus because the queen had to work under the advisor for the summer. I hated being on campus because it was boring, and it was a ghost town. I was able to escape the ghost town briefly because I had to attend an HBCU Leadership Conference.

This conference was filled with student leaders from all HBCUs across the nation. I had a blast there and connected with some amazing people. There was nothing but black excellence there: an experience that I will truly never forget.

As soon as I got back to school, I had an ant infestation in my room, and I woke up covered in them. I reported it the first time and they tried to say that they didn't see any. I broke out over time, and the rash was horrible. I tried not to go to the hospital because I no longer had insurance, and I did not have enough money to pay for a visit. Instead, I used home remedies, but nothing was working. I suffered for about a month because I didn't want to kick out that money again. I swallowed my pride and went to the emergency room in the same town as my university. They had misdiagnosed me before, so I was reluctant to go there again. They basically tried to tell me I had Shingles, and it blew my mind. I was already losing my mind from being isolated on campus, but being told that I had something that would jeopardize my ability to fulfill the responsibilities of my title broke me all the way down. I was in pain daily, but I prayed and fasted for better results. I was reading the book of Job during this time, so I knew that this was only a test. I also went to the doctor back home in Florence, and she told me the breakout was because of an allergy and gave me the proper medicine.

That scare brought me closer to God than ever before. He had to humble me and catch my full, undivided attention before the school year. I never prayed and fasted before like that in my life. It had to happen. When the school year began, everything was back to normal.

However, my queen advisor was slowly showing her true colors. Over time, I learned that she was vindictive, manipulative, and jealous. I would think everything was fine until I received calls from students warning me that she just called them trying to get dirt on me. She would call them in class, asking them if I still deserved to have my title. I was shocked because she would do nothing but smile in my face. This was only the first week of school. My birthday was the following week. I walked in her office on my birthday, and all of her staff was complimenting me. This witch comes out of her office and says,

"Mhm, this dress is inappropriate for school, and that is entirely too much makeup. I should make you go back to your dorm and change. I mean, it's not bad, it's just too much." She sounded like a hater to me and her co-workers did not follow her up.

That night was my 21st birthday, and I had a private kickback with my "closest friends." I was dancing and tipsy by myself at my friend's house, and one of my friends recorded it. Two months later, my queen advisor retrieved the video. I have no idea how, but that let me know that everyone who was invited to the kickback was not my friend. Of course, she tried to hang it over my head. She tried to convince others that I was an unfit queen, but I was dancing on my 21st birthday!!! Nothing explicit was shown in the camera, but it was the only thing she could use against me. Luckily, the vice president had my back. He just saw a STUDENT "turnt up" for her 21st birthday, and he told me to watch who I called my friends.

Of course, my advisor was infuriated. Every other week, I was in the office being accused of working the door at a strip club and saying I was going to get my mom to beat her up. Silly stuff, but nah, my mom was ready to throw the hands; however, she allowed me to handle her in my own way. My advisor sent me to the vice president's office again for sitting in the university king's lap for a picture in hopes that my crowning ceremony would be canceled. She was also showing the picture to people around campus trying to stir up drama. Even though the vice president was stern, he honestly saw past her petty attempts and allowed me to have the coronation of my dreams.

At the coronation, I came down from the ceiling, and the majority of the songs were by Beyoncé. My advisor would not allow me to be great in other areas, but it was still a memorable night. She did plenty more that was just as horrible, like trying to prevent me from having events for the students, holding my crown hostage in her office, and attempting to snatch my crown off during homecoming. But, my book is not about her. I just wanted to give you all an idea of what I was experiencing while trying to complete a senior thesis, class work, queen duties, my organization, and my senior packet all at once.

Later that year, I almost fought our student body president because he hated my king, and, because I was associated with him, he always had our names in his mouth. As the university's queen, I did not appreciate my name being tarnished every week, and I got tired of it.

The fact that the student body president was also always under my queen advisor left an even worse taste in my mouth about him.

But, I am thankful for my friend who escorted me out of the room because I would have lost my title due to fighting. I was completely out of character that day. I went straight to my king's room and repented with him because of our responses to the taunting. He had stepped out of character one week earlier, too, by punching a student, but later found out that the student set him up. The student had provoked him on purpose so he could record his reaction and get him into trouble. That was so lame. As a result, I went home almost every weekend to avoid drama and to maintain my mental stability.

Christmas break was heaven for me even though I spent the majority of it working on my thesis. We did not have Wi-Fi at home either, and every time I went to the library it was acting up. Starbucks became bae, and I went there pretty often.

On New Year's Eve in 2017, my friend and I wanted to go to church and turn up afterwards. Judge us, go ahead, but keep reading. We didn't know of any churches in the area we were heading to, so I asked a mentee of mine for suggestions, and he sent me two flyers. We chose one church only because they had a comedian on the flyer, and we were two goofballs.

We went to church and it blessed us to the point of no return. We did not even want to go out afterward, and we didn't. We went to sleep at my friend's house down the street and went back to the same church the next morning. That day we rededicated our lives to Christ, and I left with the gift of the Holy Ghost with evidence of speaking in tongues. We may have been addicted at this point because we heard about the revival that week and came back. We drove an hour there and back each time. That day, we decided to introduce ourselves to the pastors. They were really nice. After we left, we read up on the pastors in our visitors' packet, and I had a couple of questions for his wife, who was the co-pastor. I had been praying for a spiritual mentor that entire week to keep me afloat, but something told me that my mentors would come to me.

The next day of revival, the pastor recognized me (as the queen of my university) in front of the entire congregation, which made me feel comfortable enough to ask my questions. I asked the first lady different questions about her calling because I knew I had one, but I had no idea what it was. That night she poured into me. She shared how she saw the hand of God over my life. Before I knew it, I was crying, and the soft music being played in the background did not help at all. I gave her a hug and left. My friend was so upset that I did not ask her to be my mentor. I told him to calm down because I felt like the pastors were going to reach out to me. I followed them on social media after our first visit to keep up with the events at the church.

I cannot lie, I did start to regret it because my friend had a point. It was a megachurch, and they have kids and grandchildren to worry about. I was a little disappointed, but I just continued on with my life. A few days later, the pastor messaged me while I was on my way back to school with a friend and asked if I had visited their other campus that was closer to me. I told him no, but I informed him that I received the gift of the Holy Ghost. I also complimented his church and how he and his wife truly inspired me.

He responded with a thankful heart and said the following:

> *"Wow! So glad to hear that. My wife and I were talking about you and how we see the hand of God on your life. Now, you didn't ask for all this extra either but though I know you have plans to leave SC, go to grad school, etc. I want you to be very intentional and deliberate about asking the Lord to order your steps and direct your path so that you stay in His will and end up where he wants you to be. This may have nothing to do with my church, but I am talking about God's plans for you and your life wherever that may be. Now that you have received the Holy Ghost, be deliberate about spending time daily, praying in the spirit (tongues), and then spending time quietly in God's presence to hear his instructions. I perceive that this is a very pivotal point in your life so you need to clearly hear God. Reach out to us if we can be of spiritual help to you."*

This paragraph made me want to change my life forever. I was in tears. The part that struck a nerve was that two complete strangers took the time out of their busy schedules to sow into my life. Now, I told God that I would live all the way right after I graduated from college…the nerve of me. Little did I know that the last semester of my collegiate matriculation would be the beginning of a serious walk with God. The pastor went on to give me their emails, and there you have it: I was granted two spiritual mentors.

As the weeks went by, I experienced "church hurt" for the first time by the church I was attending while going to school. I quickly noticed that during the service, the pastor literally spent the most time on the tithes and offering part. Not only did they count the money as soon as you placed it down, but they gave the pastor a total immediately, and it was NEVER enough. On one particular Sunday the pastor said, "I'm the one who prays for y'all and answers the phone when y'all call, but y'all give money to each other before y'all give it to me." Then he started calling people by name to give again. He did something similar the other Sundays, but I did not have the Holy Ghost at the time. Once I did, it unsettled my spirit and I could not ignore it. I mean, I had planned on being baptized there and everything, but after speaking with my spiritual mentor and friend, I learned that I did not want to get baptized by a spirit I did not agree with. I never returned to that church.

Ironically, the church I visited for New Year's had a campus in the city where my college was as well. I went there and it was very similar, but smaller with different pastors. I started going there on Sundays and invited my mentees to come with me. One morning, the pastors from the main campus told me to download a money app and sent me the most money I had ever been given in my entire life. I cried all day just thinking about it. My heart was so warm. Words literally could not express to them how appreciative I was. Every day I was praying in my heavenly language and spending time with God. I made sure I tithed off of that blessing as well.

It became really awkward because the students would walk up and say there was something different about me. The friends I already had automatically stopped inviting me to parties and it hurt to the core. I knew God was in the midst of it all though. It was very hard from once being the life of the party to not being invited to the party at all. I did not tell my friends about my life altering event because I wanted it to be noticeable through my actions. It was indeed noticeable because for about a month, I was treated like a red-headed stepchild.

The pastors then connected me with their daughter who was around my age who also decided to take her walk with God seriously. She explained to me that she went through the same thing with friends. She encouraged me to pray for like-minded friends. At that time, I had three, but I met people I was able to pray with along the way.

Two months after this, I was accepted into the sorority I had wanted to be a part of since I was four years old. I was not nearly as financially prepared this time around. Many people donated for it to be so last minute, but I paid out of pocket for most of it. I did not have the same support. My own cousin backed out of writing my letter again because she believed the rumors about me. I did not allow this deterrent situation to defeat me because I knew that God did not bring me to my senior year without being able to scratch that accomplishment off my college bucket list. It was a nerve-racking and exhausting process.

Ironically, my queen week was the same week of the process. I would host forums on and off campus and run into our meetings like a chicken with my head cut off. (I was supposed to have my queen week five months prior, but my queen advisor tried to make the students loathe me by limiting my outreach toward them. My six-page letter to the administration about her finally freed my events, but the timing was terrible).

Surprisingly, I stood up in front of all 88 of my soon to be sorority sisters and humbly apologized for their negative impression of me because of the rumors. I explained the process I encountered with security and even the first lady of the university. I cleared up every rumor as professionally as I knew how and sat down. Some believed me and some did not, but I felt relieved and that was really all that mattered.

On March 5, 2017, I became the number of perfection and completion (7) in my favorite sorority. I received so many gifts and love. I smiled in front of my haters who were a part of the same sorority but did not want me to get in because they said it would make me cocky. I stood on top of those same girls who tried to fight me on many different occasions. I even destroyed the rumor from back home that claimed I was supposedly "blackballed"

from the entire sorority. Later on, every girl, who gave me a hard time during this process, apologized to me.

That was the year my favorite scripture became 2 Corinthians 12:9: *"But he said to me, 'My grace is sufficient for you, for my power is made perfect in weakness. Therefore I will boast all the more gladly about my weaknesses, so that Christ's power may rest on me."* I was weak mentally, physically, and emotionally my senior year, but God's grace sustained me through it all, and He made me even stronger.

The night before graduation, I was on my knees praying for God to order my steps. I was anxious, nervous, and overwhelmed because I found out that the woman who offered me a full-ride to the college I had told everyone I was going to attend was fired. Of course, the employees after her did not follow-up with this process, and I was back to square NONE. I was thinking, "How could a girl who was successful in college be unsuccessful afterward?"

I just kept praying and worshipping throughout the night. My friend from home came to stay with me, and he almost cursed me out until he saw what I was doing because he was trying to sleep. The next day I graduated Summa Cum Laude with the highest grade point average in the entire Department of Social Sciences. This was a blessing because I skipped class sometimes to take naps, to get piercings, and to go shopping.

This was the ultimate slay. My grades dropped a little my senior year, and I did not keep my 4.0, but my 3.9 grade point average showed everyone firsthand how God's power was perfected in my weakness.

Upon graduating, the Holy Spirit continued working in me. I stopped cursing, partying all the time, and giving in to all fleshly desires (two years celibate). I cannot make this up because all of these things naturally left my flesh. I literally decided that I wanted everything that God had planned for me without penalty or delay.

Although my parents did not throw me a graduation party, I accomplished something that the generational curse said I could not. God is my biggest fan, and I am my own mascot. I pushed through the concrete so that I could begin blossoming. Everyone thought the concrete buried me, but they did not know I was a seed that found an alternative route through the cracks. It had to happen.

THE BLOSSOMING

***"The Lord had said to Abram, 'Go from your country, your people and your father's household to the land I will show you. I will make you into a great nation, and I will bless you; I will make your name great, and you will be a blessing.'"* Genesis 12:1-2**

A week after graduating, I received a call stating that I was selected for an internship in Washington, DC. They covered all traveling and housing expenses. Most importantly, it was a PAID internship. Thank God I was not going to be working at home for the summer with my ex-boyfriend's mom. I still love her dearly but hearing about him every day would have driven me crazy. She did not want me to go. My mother did not want me to go either because she didn't want to be alone. My dad was mainly worried about me being a country girl in the city.

I had also just met this young preacher whom I was really attracted to, but he was not willing to try long distance. Literally everyone was against me going, but I kept getting signs that I needed to go. Not only did we not have Wi-Fi or air at my uncle's house, but I still did not have a car, which would've made getting to work a hassle. We moved with my uncle to another part of the hood, but in a much bigger house. I remember crying tears of joy because this was by far the best bedroom I ever had. However, without air or Wi-Fi or a car, being there, would have been almost unbearable.

I was seeking godly wisdom but wasn't sure exactly what move I should make. Ironically, the churches I visited, near school and back home, were focusing on these "*Faith Voyages*" and "*Taking New Territory*" series. These series were so timely. They said that you çannot expect different results by doing the same thing over and over again. They promoted radical faith to break routines. They also stressed that familiarity resulted in complacency and how God is too big for that.

That really hit me, and that day I went up to the altar for prayer regarding my decision, and the pastor prayed for me. I did not tell the pastor why I went up for prayer, but he hit every nail on the head. I wrote down the prayer as soon as I got back to my seat. He said. "*Don't try to please anyone. God has closed doors just so others could open. Cast out fear because greatness is in you. God already has a path set out for you.*" That was the confirmation that I needed.

Though my mom did not want to hear it, she knew that it had to be done. I consulted other people for guidance, but that prayer from the pastor stuck to me. As I prepared to leave, I had to stand up to everyone who did not want me to go. I believe I fasted for an answer regarding this as well. Everything was being thrown at me in an attempt to get me to stay, but I finally stood firm in my decision even though the deterrent comments struck a nerve every time. The week before, I was extremely nervous, but I refused to recoil. Now I had a point to prove.

IT HAD TO HAPPEN

As soon as I got to the airport, I wanted to turn around and go home. My parents were at the airport, and I teared up as soon as I walked in. Never in my twenty-one years of life had I stepped foot on a plane, and unfortunately, I was alone for my first flight. That's right, the "thug" from the East Side was shaking in her boots at that very moment. My dad was laughing at me, and my mom was nervous. They had flown multiple times because my dad used to work at the airport but quit before I was born. They set me up.

I stepped foot on that plane and was too cheap to download Apple Music, so I turned on one of the church's Podcasts. The sermon was entitled "Going Where You Haven't Gone Before." I had a window seat, and I looked out the entire time. I was admiring God's creation. When I felt the turbulence, I just started praying. Thankfully, the flight was only 30 minutes because I had to switch to a larger airport. My anxiety was definitely doing the Crip walk. I had no idea what was next, so I called my dad. He told me to find the schedule, and it would tell me which gate to go to.

I checked in and then I went to Burger King. I did not let my suitcase from my grasp, and I was struggling because it was bigger than me and I had an over-packed carry-on (I am learning to pack lighter the older I get). The next flight was an hour long and it was nighttime. When I landed, I had to figure out how to get to the shuttle bus and that took another hour. The driver dropped me off on the side of the road and drove off. I honestly thought he was going to help me get my bags out and walk me in, but the southern hospitality clearly ended in South Carolina.

As soon as I got out, I thought a puppy ran past me, but it was a WHOLE rat. I screamed and ran up to the door. Of course, it was locked, but luckily a girl who was struggling too was outside with me. I was miserable, and I LOVED her company. We finally got in touch with someone and got settled in at 2:00 am. I walked in on a Mexican girl who was asleep. After being at an HBCU for so long, I was not sure how this was going to go, but the first day she explained to me how the whole "brown" community was oppressed and how she hated white privilege and the 45th. I told her we were going to get along just fine, and we did.

My first day of work in Washington, DC was a culture shock. The fast pace and underground metro almost took me out. I tried not to look afraid, but I was terrified. My roommate felt the same, but she actually screamed in the metro. We walked in and were stationed in our offices.

On the first day, we saw a woman sticking her ear to the door across from us. She was definitely eavesdropping, and she busted in the door to ask if they were talking about her. The other interns and I were in disbelief, but we learned very early how toxic the environment was.

Later that day, we met with the director. I made a lasting first impression on him after discussing the crabs in a barrel effect that African Americans tend to portray. My point was that it stemmed from slavery because masters turned slaves against each other when they appointed overseers for the plantation. All the slaves strived to become an overseer because all they had to do was tell the other slaves what to do. Even if it meant selling out their own kind, it would allow them to have a better chance of survival. Slavery ended, but the mentality remained.

The director asked me if someone told me that, but I explained my outlook on that situation. He was utterly impressed. He also came from very humble beginnings, and that just made him love me more. That was my grandpa in my head, but he did not know it.

The job was cool. I worked with a guy who was old enough to be my father and a girl who was younger than I am. That girl hated us because we dressed professionally, we articulated well, and we both belonged to Greek organizations. To say the least, she was pretty hood and had grown complacent with what she knew. One day she told our boss that we left her out of the group project and that we thought we were better than her. Our boss was older, and he was in the same fraternity as my coworker. My discernment picked up that they knew each other and after lurking on Facebook I found a picture of them. I never voiced that I knew it because they kept their relationship strictly professional, and I sat back and observed their interaction. After we were called into the office due to her snitching, my coworker was pissed and voiced how dumb she was because he and our boss had been friends for over 15 years. I pretended to be shocked after he revealed that information, but in my head, I was screaming, "I KNEW IT."

We then decided to talk to the girl because we were all in the same office and she said nothing. My coworker literally started reading her for filth (going off), but I decided to stop him and approached her calmly with an apology. I told her that if she felt like we were superior, that was not the case because age means nothing in the corporate world. She started crying, and we were literally so confused. Then, when she started getting angry almost immediately after crying, we discovered that she had serious issues. I offered to give her a hug, but she called us fake and told me not to touch her and stormed out. Meanwhile, all the adults were in the hallway listening and got busted eavesdropping when she snatched the door open. They were sooo messy. My coworker and I were a little worked up because we really were being genuine, but we were really annoyed with the futile drama she caused. Her motive was for us to get in trouble and she thought she had succeeded.

The very next day, she went to another coworker instead of our boss. The worker then went to the director and made it appear like our boss was not doing his job. Our boss, in return, was petty and sent her home for the inappropriate attire that she's worn every day. Karma was proven to be real because no one was a fan of her after that. She was only hurting herself.

I literally started killing this girl with kindness, well, kind of. I wrote quotes on the dry erase board, but they were literally about her. One of them was from a singer named Lauryn Hill: *"How you gone win if you ain't right within?"* She snitched about that, too, and the boss told me to not even look at her because she was irking his last nerve with all of the snitching. I was still cordial with her because I recognized that this was not a natural battle. Everyone loved me in the office, so I knew this was nothing but an act of jealousy, which is demonic. With this in mind, I recalled her telling me that she did not go to church or believe in God "like that" because it was her personal preference.

I knew this was a battle in the spiritual realm and my friend in the office was aware as well. He did nothing but play gospel music in our office, and I anointed it with oil. We also allowed her to run the group project, and we had zero input. We allowed her to do most of the work, too. Long story short, we did not present the project, and it was a complete waste of HER time.

Nonetheless, my summer in DC was the best summer I have ever had. DC happy hours were a big thing apparently, AND they were cheap. Every day after work we got lit and full. On Thursdays, we went to the club for free wings, pasta, and $3 drinks.

My roommate and I never had an issue, and my other group of friends were lit…sometimes too lit. I even introduced one friend to God and black churches (she was mixed but was adopted by white parents). My favorite memory was celebrating my birthday early. I had over 20 people there, which consisted of my family, friends, and my mentor from work. The chef came out to meet me, and, of course, he was flirting. But most importantly, he blessed the table with complimentary appetizers and kept wings coming all night. They also brought my cake out to my favorite twerking song, and I twerked on an 80-year-old Italian man who worked there…don't ask. Afterward, we sang karaoke at a gay bar with feathers everywhere, and we literally sang our souls out. I will never forget it.

I even cut all of my hair off to go natural. For me, it symbolized a new chapter I was entering in my life. I was eager to see the woman I was going to evolve into post-graduation. I wanted something to grow with me, so I chose my hair. It was really a spur of the moment decision. I always had really long hair, and people always recognized me with the same basic wrap style that I had worn for years. I never was big on weave, so I chopped it off. An internship friend down the hall chopped it off while she was on the phone with her dad the entire time. And no, I did not cry. I came close though.

I even finessed a role in a BET commercial after submitting my photos on Instagram. It was for Dr. Scholl's and we were on a rooftop working out in 90-degree weather for hours, but the opportunity was amazing, especially since they aired it.

I also met this guy from my school whom I did not know personally. He LOVED my hair. He was in the internship as well. We started talking, and he was a true gentleman. We hung out every day, and he even met my family in DC. He had a girlfriend back in our home state, but she cheated. He even cried in my arms explaining it. I was upset that he did not tell me, but I developed feelings for him. I even prayed for his healing and forgiveness toward her.... crazy right? I did not want to be the reason their relationship ended, and I knew I could not compete with a four-year relationship. This was literally the only girl he had ever been with in his life. We hung out a lot, and that is what I felt bad about. We were not physically involved, but our emotions were because we had an awesome connection. We even went to church together. I started falling back even though it hurt me to do so.

The following week he told me he broke up with his girlfriend. I had mixed emotions because I really liked him, but I felt like I was the primary cause of his breakup. He assured me that I was not. I did not want to be a rebound, and I also did not want him to think that spending a lot of time with a female like he did with me was acceptable if we started dating. He understood, and I believed that he was an honest person. We picked back up where we left off. The only difference was that he started paying for the outings we went on.

Over time, he said the "L" word, and I honestly could not say it back. We were literally great friends, and I liked him; but saying that word was really tough for me. You would think that he would have stopped saying it after that, but he didn't. He said it every day after that. I was still celibate at this time, and I did not say it back until the last day of the internship.

Professionally, things were going great, too. I was promised a full-time job after the internship ended. I was the only intern asked to come back, but I did not know how bittersweet it would be until I returned to work for them. I was really sad when it was time to return home, but I was ready to leave my job. The adults in the office did not like how the director praised me at the going away social for the interns. It was mainly the white woman trapped inside a black woman's body. She was racist against her own kind and was upset that the director did not have the same words for the mixed intern in our office that he barely knew. The people were psycho in that office.

My anxiety went crazy all over again when it was time to leave because this was only my second time on a plane, and I forgot what the process was like because the internship was three months long. I was like a deer caught in headlights all over again, but I made it home. Bald and all. My parents hated my hair, but more people liked it on Instagram so I did not care…I'm kidding. I did get more juice once I cut my hair, and I cannot marry my parents so whose opinion really matters at this point?

Moving right along, I was depressed for a whole month and a half because of the tedious process I had to endure upon my arrival for full-time employment. The federal government is nothing to play with because the job process is very tedious. I would wake up early to take my mom to work, swim, workout, and go to church. I repeated that with the exception of going out to eat with the same friend every week.

My 22nd birthday was the only thing that was exciting while I was home. I went to North Carolina to visit my best friend (my king) from college. He had music and sangrias made for me as soon as I stepped in the door. We went to a paint and sip class, the club, kayaking, brunch, and another club. At least five other friends joined, and he threw me a day party on the last day. We had mimosas, chicken, rice, gravy, macaroni, and collard greens. He even baked me a cake. An epic weekend, indeed. Then, I went right back to being depressed. We STILL had no wifi, no air downstairs (where my room was), and still no car. I felt like a WHOLE pilgrim.

I checked in with my mentor in DC every week to see when I could start. In the meantime, I contacted a friend of a friend who agreed that I could occupy their living room for a small fee because DC was so expensive. I had been conversing with him weekly to see what I needed to bring and to find out where he lived. He kept saying I was more than welcome to come after his brother leaves. Two weeks later, I got cleared, and he gave me the same response. At this time, I told him I was preparing to leave, and I just agreed to sleep on my air mattress until his brother left.

I went to my high school to fill out extra paperwork for my job, and I started packing. I was anxious. I purchased holy oil, and I drove an hour and 20 minutes to get prayer from the church that I went to for New Years. Two members there also took me out to dinner and prayed with me as a going away gift before I returned home.

Then, the day arrived. My dad pulled up at 6:00 am to take me to Washington, DC. I already had mixed emotions because my prospective roommate would not answer the phone or text back. I had no address to give my dad, so I just gave him my cousin's address in Maryland. Meanwhile, I was crying and freaking out in the back seat silently. I texted my other cousin who is a couple years older than I am, and I asked her if I could spend the night for one night until my friend came to get me the next day. At first, she said yes, but then she suggested that I stayed with my cousin I intended on staying with from the beginning.

I did not want to ask that cousin because she had simply done so much for me over the years, but my cousin already called her and told her that I was coming. No loyalty at all. I was crying and praying that my roommate would text back, but six hours later I was pulling into my cousin's yard. She greeted us with love as she always did, and my dad unpacked the truck and left. I was happy to be there, but not under those circumstances.

I started work in two days, but I had no idea how I was going to get there. I texted another friend that I met at the HBCU conference, and he was willing to help me out until I could get back on my feet. But, he lived in a house with five other boys, and I was NOT feeling that. At that point, I had to be honest with my cousin and tell her what was going on. Luckily, she let me stay. I woke up extra early to take a seven-minute walk to the bus stop. I, then, rode the bus for an hour to the metro station and spent an hour on the metro to get to downtown DC. After all that traveling, my first day of work was cool.

I literally did nothing during the internship, and it was the same environment when I returned. My internship friend (the grown man) was still there, but everyone's attitude shifted from when I was there for the summer. The only people who were excited to see me was the director and my mentor. My mentor told me that they saw me as a threat since I was on their level. I decided to keep my communication to a minimum at that moment because I saw a glimpse of their behavior toward each other over the summer.

Unfortunately, the director was demoted due to someone in the SAME office. That is when everything started to go downhill. It was every man for themselves AND their home-girls. Everyone started going into the new director's office trying to get assigned different projects so they could secure their positions, including my friend from the internship.

I found out over time that people started lying on me, saying that I did not get to work on time, even though I was there before everyone. Everything in me wanted to plead my case, but my mentor was doing it for me. Furthermore, something in me was telling me to remain still. I anointed my office and the hallway on the first day. I really wanted God to make this decision for me, so I did not lift a finger. My commute seemed only to worsen. My anxiety, with multiple strangers on the city bus and metro, really consumed me on a daily basis. Some people were mentally ill and did weird things on there. One woman hissed at this man because he did not give her money. All the while, I was listening to the podcasts from the church again. I had also finally decided to download Apple Music, so I could blend in with the city people.

I only listened to gospel because I was really starting to go under. Gospel music is my favorite and it calms me. I stayed with my cousin for two weeks, and the second week, I house-sat while my cousins went out of the country. This was good because I did not feel like too much of a burden. While they were gone, I fed all eight animals twice a day. She left me her Lexus, but I did not drive to the metro or work because the traffic was nothing like South Carolina. And I did not want to try it out in her car. I only went to Bible study and Sunday morning service in her car.

I also tried out for a modeling agency downtown. Of course, they loved my southern charm, but a midget was the last thing they were looking for. At least they let me down easy, and a guy model asked for my number afterward.

My mom always mentioned that my 77-year-old cousin would love if I moved in with her. I was elated because not only did she live an hour away from my job, but she and her late husband also loved and spoiled me ever since I was younger. On the day when it was time for me to move in, she made a whole 180. She did not answer the phone for me, and she told my mom that she was not used to having company because she liked being alone. I literally broke down when my mom told me that. I did not understand why my family was not as supportive as I thought they would be.

With all of this going on, I was becoming even more stressed out because I LOATHED feeling like a burden. I was also tired of feeling unstable because I had no idea where I was going to lay my head next. When my cousin dropped me off, she felt bad while she was helping me unload my things because my elderly cousin did not have Wifi, and she refused to turn on the air conditioning. I gave my cousin a big hug and stayed upstairs the entire time.

I took an Uber every time I needed to go somewhere. My cousin refused to even go to church with me. She criticized my hair, wardrobe, and presence on a daily basis while having my picture on her refrigerator. I did not understand her; I was more of a help than a hindrance. When I was interning in DC, she begged for me to come visit, and I even went with her to get her first tattoo at 77 years old. She also paid for food for me and the four other friends that I had with me. I offered to pay her something for allowing me to stay, but she would not take it.

Although my cousin lived only an hour away from my job, the commute was not that much better because she lived in the back of her neighborhood, which consisted of really steep hills. It took me 11 minutes to get to the bus stop, 30 minutes to get to the metro, and 30 minutes to get to work. It was progress, but learning the new process with new strangers had me stressed once again. I never had to be so alert in my life.

I did not have many friends in DC. The guy who dropped the L bomb from the internship was only two hours away but did a complete 180 on me. Not only was I barely hearing from him, but he refused to allow me to come see him and vice versa. Clearly, there was someone else and that hurt because I felt like that was when I needed him the most. He would never admit it, but his entire demeanor had changed. I was more frustrated than anything because I could not wait to see him again.

There was one girl I met from the internship who was cool, but we were completely different people. So, we only hung out occasionally. However, I was able to experience many HBCU homecomings with the few that I did know. While in DC, I visited

Howard University, the University of Maryland Eastern Shore (not a HBCU), Lincoln University, Bowie State University, and Virginia State University. I also met a young black girl on the metro. She came up to me and asked me if I knew about god the mother/the bride. She showed me scriptures and invited me to a waffle social at her church. I gave her my email, but after we got off the metro we walked into the same building. When we found out that we worked in the same building, we were astonished and met up for lunch and exchanged contact information. She was really nice and kept asking me during the week if I was still going to the waffle social. I told her yes. She was only two metro stops away, so I figured I would not be too far from my cousin's house.

However, she neglected to tell me that we were going to a different campus, which was 45 minutes away. Nonetheless, it was church, so I got in the car with her. We literally sat in silence because she did not like listening to music, but I could not take it. I started playing gospel music, but she did not know any of it. I asked who her favorite gospel artists were, but she could not answer that either. That was a red flag. She also decided to do her makeup on the interstate while driving with her knee. (Now some of you reading this may do that, but it is NOT okay by any means, especially if other people are in the car with you crazies).

We finally arrived at the church and my spirit felt funny. It was raining, and a group of girls came OUTSIDE to greet me and they had no idea what personal space meant. They were in my face with a dazed stare welcoming me and hugging me. Afterward, we finally made it in the church where people were praying with long white veils on their head staring into a blank space not moving.

I asked if they were going to the waffle social, and she told me it depends on what time they got done praying. In my head, I was freaked out, but I was also thinking "Wow, these people love the Lord so much that they are willing to skip out on waffles to pray." Do not judge me. We finally sat down, and we had a brief Bible lesson about the Passover, which was normal until they played a recruitment video immediately afterward. During this recruitment video, the videographer was recording me the entire time.

The video explained how their church was founded by a Korean man, and how his wife basically believed that when God comes back, it will be in the form of the Korean man who founded the church. She was the “god the mother” that the girl mentioned to me at the metro stop. The video showed how they won awards for their community service everywhere except in the United States and showed the hundreds of campuses across the country. I looked over and the videographer was still focused on me. I tried not to have a major reaction to the video, since I was being recorded. But if everyone there was a member, I was confused as to why a recruitment video was played.

There was also a photographer who came to our table at least four times to take pictures of us. I was a little freaked out, but I was only there for a free meal. We finally ate, but before I took a bite I said a strong prayer with tongues and all. The food was absolutely delicious. I am sorry, but if you did not know, food is my ultimate weakness, ESPECIALLY if it is free.

While we were wrapping up our meal, the girl tells me that we were going to go to the back for another lesson. Please do not get me wrong, I love the Lord with ALL of my heart, but I already went to church that morning. Do not forget that we just had a lesson before we ate. Now she wanted to have another? I politely told her that we had to work in the morning, and I had the "itis". She thought I was kidding and mentioned that we worked together, so she out of all people knew what time we should get back.

I followed her down the hall and people who were in the waffle social were in the rooms studying as well. Her friend who was eating at the table with us was standing at the dry erase board. I sat down and her friend wanted to teach me MORE about the church. In a nutshell, they told me I was going to hell because I went to church on the Sabbath day, which was Sunday. They even had a dictionary and history book to try to justify, but I knew that the Bible was one book that could stand alone.

They told me that there was a father god and mother god, and they made me read scriptures aloud as if I was a four-year-old. They also attended church three times on Saturday, which results in them being there all day. After a while, I started speaking in tongues under my breath, and I stopped turning to the scriptures when they told me to. The girl reached over and started turning to the scriptures for me. I read with disinterest, and my whole mood shifted. I felt as if they were going to sacrifice me at that point. My mom called, and they asked me to put my phone away.

That was the moment I started to call an Uber, but I was almost an hour away. The ride would have been crazy expensive. I thugged it out until the end without receiving anything that was trying to be taught to me. We finally got in the car to leave, and she asked me if I was coming with her next Saturday. I politely said that I would have to do more research, and she responded aggressively saying that they taught me everything that I needed to know. I had enough. I called my mom and conversed with her for 30 minutes and did the same with my dad immediately afterward so that I could be occupied the entire ride back.

She tried to have lunch with me the next day, but I told her that I had work to do in the office. I told one of my coworkers about my experience, and she went on YouTube. There were hundreds of testimonials on how it was a cult and how people have lost contact with their loved ones because of this cult. The people in the testimonials proceeded to say how they believe that it is selfish to bring kids in the world because the world is going to end soon, and I also remembered how the girl mentioned that she did not want children even though she was married. The testimonials also said that they do not tell people everything about their beliefs until they get them in the church, and they try to manipulate people and make them feel guilty. I shook the entire time. My coworker was terrified and said I should be glad they did not sacrifice me like a lamb in the Bible. I agreed. I told my parents what had happened to me and my mom cussed me slam out.

My dad was also really concerned and unhappy. I get it, but allow me to ask this question. If a peer around your age asked you to attend a waffle social at their CHURCH, wouldn't you join them? Come on, it sounds so innocent. Anyway, the girl later popped up at my metro stop again, and I spoke but did not sit next to her. After a while, she left me alone, but I was constantly watching my back.

As time passed, I met a great, loyal friend at my church after that. She was African and really genuine. It all started when I asked her if I could give my tithes online at church. From then on, she took me under her wing. She introduced me to her friends, and we all clicked naturally. I began embracing my African culture, and I was learning more about it. They even taught me African dances and introduced me to some awesome African songs. This girl helped me move into the room I rented, AND she spent my first night there with me on an air mattress. Now that's loyalty. She took me to her college homecoming, and we had a blast. She also prayed with me on one of my lowest days, which happened to be on HER birthday. I am so blessed to have met such a loyal person with a heart of gold. God showed me what a real friend looked like so that I would not regret losing the others. It had to happen.

Before I found a place, my housing search in DC was tragic, but, thankfully, my cousins were realtors and they caught a man claiming a house that was not his. My cousins had special access to a website and contacted the rightful owners before they could scam me out of my money. Then, there was a girl around my age who gave me a tour of an entire house TWICE and even invited me to her church. She took my application fee and tried to rush a down payment before I moved in because she was going out of town, but I was finally catching on to DC people. This girl staged the home in which no one lived. She also changed things around the second time to make it seem as if four other girls really lived there. I was confused because out of all of the four times I had been to the house, no one was there. She always had to come to meet me. I never heard from her again, but she did scam me out of the $50 application fee. There were other cases where I left work to look at many different rooms, but I was not feeling those either.

There was even a woman trying to put me in a basement with no windows. I was about to lose my mind. One lady also took me on a tenant interview to her church to see if I was suitable for her room. Now I went because I actually knew people who went to the church, and she had Jesus all over her home. I know what you are thinking: I still have not learned my lesson. But, even the Christians were out there trying to make a dollar. Her room was overpriced and her house and car smelled like strong perfume and booty meat. I was suffocating in her car on the way to church, guys. I could not do it.

Randomly, I landed a speaking role in another BET commercial endorsing Universal Studios. (Not only did they love me, but out of six other people, they only used me for BOTH commercials). So, I met a guy on set who I was actually mean to because he talked and swore a lot, but he loved me for some reason. He talked to the landlord next door to him for me, and he was willing to rent a room out to me that was 30 minutes from my job. It sounded too good to be true because it also was in my budget. The room was large, and I only had to share the bathroom with one other person, which was the landlord's sister. I just knew the landlord could not mistreat us since his sister lived in the home. He even used the Lord as his witness and said he had a daughter my age, so he would not mistreat me because he believed in karma. He told me that they had Wi-Fi and that he was getting the water pressure fixed.

But, before I moved in, my mentor checked with my job to see if I was going to be laid off, and the interim director told her that I had nothing to worry about. So, I proceeded to move in. As far as work, I able to attend The 40th Black Women's Agenda during the Congressional Black Caucus Conference for free. I saw so many celebrities, and black girl magic was everywhere. The director from work even went out of her way to speak to me, but I am pretty sure it was only because she was the only white woman there out of thousands of black women. They also had me drafting a proposal for the ambassador's program they wanted to jumpstart. I came up with brilliant ideas, and they even told me to choose five universities I was interested in visiting for the recruitment of the internship. I rocked the meeting, and I was confident in my position until one of the black women was fired without notice. Then, I was on pins and needles squeezing my cheeks and not the ones on my face.

The following week, two other people were let go. However, I was not afraid because the director told my mentor that I was fine. Randomly, the woman who put me over the program told my mentor that she did not want to give me the bed she had at her house, and that she did not know how I knew she had one that she wanted to give away in the first place. I am not a prophet, guys: this lady clearly came to my office offering me the bed set, and since I did not have one yet, I said yes. I did remind her of it once, but once my mentor told me the unnecessary lie she told, I never mentioned it again. I started to watch her as well.

Meanwhile, I discovered that the landlord's sister was a lunatic. Not only did she not want to move any of her things in the bathroom or the kitchen so I could store my belongings, but she also did not know the definition of personal space. She would trap me in the bathroom while I was doing my hair to sell me things and talk my head off. She would interrupt me while I was on the phone to do silly things, like ask me to pet her dog so it could get used to me. She was in her forties and lonely. I get it, but the day she followed me in my room trying to sell me plastic drawers, I was over it. I had to let the landlord know that she was overbearing, but he knew his sister. He laughed, apologized, and handled it. After that she hated me. She started leaving urine in the toilet. She also yelled at me for hanging my towel in the bathroom but hung her panties up. Also, the first day I was there, she told me not to leave food out because it attracted roaches, but she started leaving dishes in the sink and her cereal boxes wide open, welcoming them to come. Her dog even pooped in front of the staircase. After all of this, we still did not have Wifi, strong water pressure, and the heat was broken during the winter.

The landlord's sister was complacent with washing with 3 droplets of water, but I was not. I released most of my stress in the shower and tub so if I was paying $800 for rent, I felt as if that was the least the landlord could do. I started to discern my roommate's pettiness and the landlord's deceitfulness. Just when I thought I made a horrible commitment, it got worse. One day at work, I was sitting in my office reading my Bible, and the worker who was a white woman trapped in a black woman's body mysteriously came in acting very friendly and asked me how I was doing.

I said I was great, and she looked at me like I was crazy and walked out. Approximately ten minutes later, I received a call saying that my contract had been terminated. They told me I had until the end of the day to vacate the premises or security would escort me out. My heart dropped, and I texted my mentor. She told me to come to her office, and that was when I broke down. She felt just as betrayed as I did because they told her that I had nothing to worry about. I was devastated because not only did I move seven hours away from home for this job, but I had also just signed a lease agreement. I spent most of that day out of the office trying to get myself together because I refused to allow anyone to see me sweat, ESPECIALLY the one who smiled in my face that morning and knew exactly what was happening.

It took everything I had not to go slap her, but she probably would have pressed charges. Later, they sent out a mass email saying that cake was on the end of the hall. I came down the hall grinning when I saw the director, "Oreo", and the lady who placed me over the program. I asked what kind of cake it was, and I leaped for joy and smiled because it was my favorite. I said thank you and walked back like being laid off did not phase me. That HURT man. I had so many mixed emotions looking at the people who betrayed me, but I HAD to kill them with kindness. I packed my things after my coworker in my office left and said my goodbyes respectfully.

Many other workers were upset because they knew my circumstances, so they started sending me job applications immediately. I wanted to respectfully approach the director and leave a lasting impression in hopes that she would change her mind, but my mentor already tried and told me that the director did not care. She said the director was nonchalant and crass. She also said she had never seen her so mean before.

I really wanted closure, but I listened to my mentor who had a pure heart from the beginning. She also told me that the lady who had me over the recruiting program told the director that she did not need me when the director asked if my position was needed. This lady had taken my proposal and claimed it as her own. More betrayal. Finally, I went to go see the director who was demoted upstairs, and he felt horrible. He did not know about any job opportunities, but he gave me

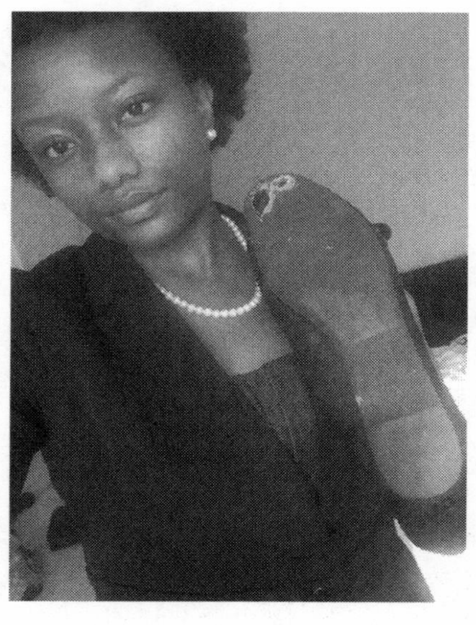

$800 for my rent the following month, and he added me on his MetroCard system so that I would no longer have to pay for transportation. I told him that he did not have to, but he insisted.

Between him and my mentor, they had me making $63,000 that year. I would have been set for the year, but during this storm, I was believing God for greater. I took the walk of shame out of my job, and even the security guards were devastated because I was able to use my southern charm to make friends with people around the entire building. The next day, the lady who told the director she did not need me anymore gave me the number to someone else's office for a job. I dressed up in my black skirt suit and black flats, that I had walked a hole into, and went in for an interview.

I took a challenging placement test. There were some things on there that they neglected to show me in computer class. I was very discouraged, but, according to the CEO of the company, I did not do as badly as I thought I had done. As she continued to speak, I was recollecting my memory. I interrupted her by asking if she was a Soror and if she had two daughters. She said yes. I told her that I was at her house on the fourth of July with my friend who is also friends with her daughter. She confirmed everything, and I was so relieved because I just knew this was God moving.

Unfortunately, the only position she had open was in Baltimore, Maryland. I could not accept it, but she did allow me to come to the office to use a computer to apply for jobs since I did not have Wifi. Occasionally, they would buy me lunch, but for the most part, they left me alone and never questioned my time there.

Next, I went to the unemployment office in the hood to file for unemployment. I was humiliated for three hours only to be told that I was not working long enough to receive benefits. **Side Note: I was embarrassed and frustrated because I grew up on welfare, and the last thing I wanted was to repeat a cycle that I have been working my whole life to end.** At the end of my visit, I met with a career counselor, and her son attended my alma mater. I thought this was God again because he was a hiring manager, and this woman really wanted to help me. I applied for the job even though I did not know anything about it. However, because I did not know anything about it, I was honest on my application and did not score high enough for my application to run across his desk. He could have told me to stretch the truth a little earlier, but that was a fail, too.

By this time, I was crying every single day. I really did not contact my friends from home to brief them on my situation. I was embarrassed and felt as if I would bounce back in no time, especially since I was continually reading my Bible. However, my little brother from church checked up on me weekly. When he called me tipsy on one of my weakest nights to randomly speak life into me, it really helped me get back on track. God definitely used him even though he was lit. He and my sister from church were trying to come visit me to cheer me up, but they could not agree on travel arrangements.

One day my African friend and I went to a restaurant, and I saw two elderly ladies with their sorority letters on. I had mine on, too, so I spoke and they were telling me how they just left their chapter meeting and that they needed more people my age. Once asked where I lived, it turned out that one of them only lived a few houses down from me. She gave me her number to reach out to her whenever I needed her. She was 87, but her mind was still intact. She lived alone so my company was always greatly appreciated. She was God-fearing, wise, and a landlord. She had a very nice basement no one lived in, but grandma was taxing people for rent. She owned about three row homes, and she did not play about her money. She loved me enough to feed me, but not enough for me to occupy her basement for only $800. She was a great counselor. I told her about my whole DC experience, and she had a scripture for everything.

Let's not forget everyone in DC had hidden motives, so of course, her grandson who was my age mysteriously popped up while I was visiting one day. We exchanged social media names, and he left. He was not my type, and I was not looking for ANYONE. I was just trying to focus on my screwed-up life. The elderly woman became my DC grandmother. She proceeded to introduce me to her daughter who also loved me. Her daughter set me up with an interview with CSPAN. A black woman interviewed me for hours, and I just knew I had the job, but that was the first time I received a "no" in my face. I could not take it much longer. I also came close to getting jobs in Virginia, but they wanted me to go door to door in DC, and I refused even though I was pretty desperate. I even applied to Forever 21 after I left those interviews, and they never called me back. I even had Uber drivers sending me links to applications.

I was depressed, but my prayers, church, and Bible kept me afloat. Moving back to my cousin's house was not an option either. I felt like I just had myself. Finally, I applied to a hiring agency. They were just as impressed with me as everyone else seemed to be, but I was already expecting a "no". I went home that night and really pressed in for an answer from God if I should stay or go home. Please be careful what you ask God for because while I was reading my Bible, a mouse came out of my closet. I lost it. I knew that I could no longer live in DC. I texted the landlord to tell him about the mouse, and he flipped on me. He said that I had too many complaints and that there were not any problems in the home until I moved there.

He even said that his sister told him that I kept food in my room and that I had too many clothes to fit in the room. First of all, I only had a bottle of hot sauce in my room. And, second of all, my clothes were still in bins because I did not have any dressers yet. That really hurt me.

I called my "friends" to see if I could spend the night with them, but that was a fail. I didn't even bother to contact my African friend because she lived too far away from me, and it was already late. However, the boy I met on the commercial set lived down the street, and he allowed me to sleep on his sofa. I know that was a bold move for me, but I was mentally done with everything. All I could do was threaten him and pray to God that he would not try anything. Ironically, it was the best sleep I ever had in DC. I woke up the next morning with a phone call from the job agency, and they were bribing me with a temporary job that was not guaranteed and I would have had to interview for it.

I was catching on to the hidden motives that northerners always had, and I realized that if I got in this position, they would benefit from it. They had three different people call me. One lady was trying to make rats seem normal which was NOT a smart tactic to get me to stay. They were literally begging me, but that day I simply told my mom to come to get me. She said that they would be there that weekend. It was that easy. That day I took half of my clothes and moved them to my grandma's house down the street. I did not want to leave my possessions in there unattended because of my crazy roommate. I also started packing.

That night, my African friend picked me up for her birthday dinner. She really wanted me to stay, but I knew that I had reached my breaking point when I broke down in her car. She literally took the time to pray for me and to ask God to order my steps. She took me back to her home and allowed me to stay in her guest bedroom, far away from the mouse. That morning I woke up and the Co-Pastor/First Lady from the church I went to on New Year's Eve texted me saying that God told her to tell me to come home, and that was the confirmation I needed. My African friend agreed as well. I told the job agency no for the last time, and when they attempted to guilt-trip me, I hung up and blocked them.

Ironically, my last day in DC was the best. My African friend rented a loft over the city and invited all of her African friends. There were around eight females and zero drama. We had already gone to the Museum of the Bible earlier that day, so the night was a pleasant continuation. That evening, we all had on white pajamas and red lipstick. It was a genuinely fun night with food, classy drinks, and laughter. That experience STILL did not make me want to stay. The next day we went to the church where I'd met her, but I left early because my family was on the way to get me. Thankfully, my roommate was not home during the moving-out process. The landlord came at the very end and promised to give me my deposit back since I only stayed for a month and four days. Do you think I ever received it? Of course not. Before I left, I slipped a piece of paper under my roommate's door with a scripture Job 4:8: *"As I have seen, those who plow iniquity and sow trouble reap the same."*

On the way back home, I had mixed emotions. I felt like a failure, and I wondered what people were going to say once they saw that I was back home. I was also content with my decision because I literally went through hell and back. I felt as if I'd endured what I could, and I knew for a fact some people would not have survived it. I counted it as a lesson. All of this had to happen because not only did it humble me, but it also made me one tough cookie. God and I became best friends during this process. Sometimes God has to break your heart to blow your mind. It had to happen.

THE SUNLIGHT

"And after you have suffered a little while, the God of all grace, who has called you to His eternal glory in Christ, will Himself restore, confirm, strengthen, and establish you." 1 Peter 5:10

On my way home, I got a text about speaking at two churches. I was able to confirm those gigs, which made me feel a little better because when I was in DC I felt like I was not pouring into anyone. I was used to helping other people because that was how I truly helped myself. In the meantime, I had my newborn niece to look at the whole way back, and I was so glad to be able to watch her grow up because I had to leave when she was only a month old. While playing with my beautiful niece, I managed to send my résumé to all of the high officials in Florence on the way back.

I also remembered that there was this woman at the church I went to for New Year's Eve who randomly approached me asking me if I had a job. At the time, I had just lost my job but was home visiting, so she wrote my email down anyway and emailed me saying how nice it was to meet me. I searched for her name and sent her my résumé as well.

I finally made it home, and I felt great. Although I was anxious, this was the first time I got to sleep peacefully in months. I also ceased my daily weeping, which felt awesome. I still did not have Wifi at home, so I applied for different jobs at my church member's house. There were not many openings in my hometown, so I also applied to jobs in nearby cities. Two days later, I received a call from the State House, an hour and twenty minutes away, asking me if I could come in for an interview the same day. Unfortunately, it was almost 5 o'clock, and I had to pick my mother up from work, so I could not go. Thankfully, the Senator did not mind driving an hour the next day to come meet me again. This was only by the grace of God. This is the job the lady from the church recommended me for, AND she was a Soror. I put on my best business suit with my kitten business heels and sped the whole way there (Sorry, Mom). When I got there, I had to go to the downtown area, and I could not find parking to save my life.

I called the Senator to let him know that I would be a few minutes late. Horrible first impression, right? I know. As soon as I parked, I turned into Will Smith trying to catch the bus in the *Pursuit of Happyness:* afro, briefcase, and all. I did not know which building he was in because his office was not in the main building. I asked around and finally met security at the desk who saw how frantic I was. They didn't stop to search me, and they told me the office number. I realized I was back in South Carolina because in DC they do not care how much of a rush you are in. They will make you step through that metal detector twice AND wand you down.

I was praying in tongues the whole way up to the top floor, and there he was. I thought he was white because of how he sounded on the phone, but a short, bald, black man who almost resembled my father stood in front of me. That was a confidence booster, but I knew that I still needed to "sell" myself. He tried to catch me slipping because he did not think that I had an extra copy of my résumé. Although he had one in front of him, he asked for another one to see how prepared I was. I whipped two copies out of my briefcase and gave him another copy. I kept a copy so that I could follow along with him. He told me to tell him about my upbringing, and I was transparent. Just like the director in DC, he, too, came from humble beginnings. He was relatable and the *solitaire* in his family as well. He asked me what was the biggest obstacle I had to overcome, and I told him about my mom being in jail my senior year of high school, not knowing that he is known for helping inmates in prison.

He was very straightforward, and I appreciated that. He asked if I had any questions, and I asked him what his pet peeves were. They were self-explanatory, but I wrote all of them down. His number one pet peeve was tardiness, so I just knew that I was not going to get the job. After the interview, he sent me downstairs, but I still did not know what that meant. Before I knew it I was discussing my start date with the clerk and receiving an offer letter.

I called the lady from the church immediately and met her in her office. I was telling her how the interview went, and she said hopefully I will get a call soon. I told her that I got the job, and she went crazy! It was still surreal to me because I was car-less and had no idea how I was going to start commuting in four days. I still had a thankful heart, though. I called my parents with the good news. Of course, they only focused on how I was going to get there. Even though my mom lived across the street from her job, she told me that I could not drive her car.

IT HAD TO HAPPEN

By this time, I was fed up with not having a car. It had been seven years of having a driver's license without EVER having a car. So, the next day, I asked my sister-in-law to go to a dealership with me. We looked at cars and got a final price on my dream car, the car that I have been longing for, for about 5 years. I fell in love with the Alien Green Kia Soul…yes, the hamster car. With the support of my sister-in-law, she encouraged me to purchase my own car without waiting for anyone. She checked out other dealerships to see if I was getting the best deal, and we went back the next day with my mom to finalize the purchase.

Everything was running smoothly until it got to the insurance. I thought that I was still on my dad's insurance, but when I called him, he said he had taken me off. I asked if he could put me back on, and he blatantly said no. I immediately became hysterical because I never asked my parents for anything, and I have been supporting myself for the longest. I was so upset because ever since middle school I worked my behind off to not be a burden on my parents, so I felt as if this was the very least my dad could do. I hung up in my dad's face and continued my meltdown until my mom told me to stop crying and that God would work it out.

I was tempted to just ask my mom for help, but she did not even have a home of her own. I knew she could not help me. The car salesman was persistent and also spoke from a spiritual standpoint. He even offered to pay for free detailing after I purchased my car. After a short while, my dad called back pissed and agreed to add me back on his insurance. He did not have to put me through all that in the first place. Ooooohh, I was stressed, y'all, but I am beyond grateful. Two years prior, my dad also bought me a car from the auction that I did not like and never got to drive because he wrecked it. He spent years trying to repair it, and I told him to bring it to the dealership the next day so that my final price could be $500 cheaper. He, then, tried to tell me to wait until the following week so he could fix it up, but I was firm in my answer, with the help of my support system, and told him to bring it the next morning. The next morning, my whole immediate family was at the dealership. I finalized my paperwork, and I took pictures with MY brand-new car.

I turned on my music, shouted, and ran around my car. I was hurt because of all of the money I had to spend, but thankful at the same time. The Bible was not lying when it states in Psalm 126:5 that, "*Those who sow with tears will reap with songs of joy.*" A dealership worker recorded my praise because he was churchy, too. Not everyone was happy for me that day, but I did not give two FUH.... futures. Sorry, that was my flesh, y'all.

After that, I picked my best friend up, and my mom drove us to the beach in my car to get seafood. I started feeling happy for myself and planned a whole celebration kickback as I was eating. I asked my friend who was a preacher if I could use his place, and he said yes! Crazy, right?

My best friend and I picked up a bottle each and headed home. On my way home I invited people, and I picked up a cheap pizza. Before I knew it, some of my line sisters, family, and best friends were gathered to celebrate my blessing. There was no greater feeling. I ended up naming my car Sevyn (my favorite number). I even had a car probate. . . you had to be there.

My first day of work was cool. It was almost Christmas, so it was a ghost town. First and foremost, I anointed my office with oil and prayed over it. Secondly, I was really hype because I had my own office, parking spot, and decal that automatically opened the gate. It was very similar to my job in DC but better. I had such a culture shock when I returned home because everyone started casually speaking to me again. In DC I was a "thug". I did not speak, and I made no eye contact. I hated who I was becoming, to be honest, but after being gullible so many times, I realized my kindness was being mistaken for weakness. AND, I AIN'T NO PUNK! Sorry.

As the days progressed, many people on my job would randomly call in or stop by to ask me how I was doing. I thought it was weird until someone came out and told me that my boss went through two other Administrative Assistants within the past six months. One woman even said that she had to go to counseling because of him. Some people even told me that if I needed to vent, they would be a listening ear. His reputation was tarnished, but I could not react off of what others said because he gave me money to buy a refrigerator and

Keurig for our office after he saw that I was using someone else's refrigerator and Keurig. He was harsh, but my queen advisor was worse. It all made sense because God was preparing me for this.

Confused, I discussed with my church member how I did not have any problems with my boss, and she told me that when you have favor, the rules do not apply to you. She said if I did not anoint my office with oil and post daily devotions in it, it could have been another way. She truly changed my perspective, so I continued to strive to be the light in the office. However, if he did start switching up on me, I would have had a discussion explaining to him that I wanted to get along with him. I did not want to conform to everyone else. I was already defending him, and I wanted to continue to do so. I also did not have to commute back home everyday because my best friend allowed me to stay with him sometimes. In return, I hired him to work in my office. Work was fun.

A week after I purchased my vehicle, I saw that the dealership manager had commented under my shouting video to challenge me.

The video was slowly but surely going viral and he told me that if I could get 6,000 likes, he would cover 6 months of my car payment. He did not know that he was dealing with a hustler. I started tagging people and contacting the media. I was even on the news endorsing the post. Three days later, I got 6,000 likes and the dealership kept their word.

A few days later I went to the Bahamas with my best friend to visit our other friend. No, I am not rich, our friend performed on cruise ships, and we got great discounts with VIP treatment. I was even able to swim with dolphins there. Meanwhile, while my life was making a whole 180, I had my DC friends praising with me because they saw just how low I was.

After this turnaround, I joined the church I visited for New Years because it changed my entire life, and it encouraged me to do whatever it took to receive everything that God had for me. I was believing God for a lot in 2018, and as a result, I decided to handle my spiritual business first. I got baptized, joined the dance ministry, and I even sowed a HUGE sacrificial seed for the first time in my life to secure my future. Now that hurt me to the core, but something inside of me had a burning desire to sacrifice that.

I can say I was booked for many different events and made the money right back with just the events alone. Just when I thought I was being unnoticed, I was honored by a school and church for my service in the community. That reminded me that I was not overlooked but becoming overbooked. God was hiding me for such a time as this. My life was finally falling into place. My blessing was not only a testimony, but it also was a blessing to others. To top it all off I was offered a full-ride to graduate school after being accepted into five different grad schools without financial aid being offered. As I mentioned earlier, I was discouraged, but I refused to sell myself short.

I actually received a prophecy from my friend that I would get a full ride. I knew that the God who blessed me with a full-ride in undergrad could do the exact same in graduate school. I did not realize that my location delayed some of the blessings, but thank God it did not deny them. God did not want me in Alabama, New Jersey, or DC. He wanted me back at home where He could use me the most, even though it was the last place I wanted to be.

I consistently receive confirmation after confirmation that home is where I am called to be. For example, one morning my friend and I were leaving a restaurant, and it was raining horribly. At the light, a hysterical teenager begged to get in our car because her car flooded, and no one would stop to help her. We let her in, and she was having a panic attack. I embraced her. There I was, holding a stranger I did not even know. She told us that there were people still beside her car that was flooding. While we sat in the car waiting on the police, I watched the water rise. I could not allow those people to drown on my watch.

Without hesitation, I dashed into the pouring rain and ran/swam toward the car. I fell shortly afterward, but something told me to keep going. I snatched their car door open and told the two men to head to my friend's car. The water was up to the dashboard in their car and started rising more once I opened the door, but the people were so shocked that they did not know what to do. Once everyone made it to my friend's car, all they could do was worry about their cars.

TOP STORY

Former Miss Claflin springs into action to aid stranded motorists during flooding

By CONNIE JOHNSON T&D Correspondent
Aug 23, 2018 1

I fussed at all three strangers and told them that their car could be replaced, but their lives could not. I told them that I wholeheartedly believed that God had better things coming to them.

I also told them that they were living sacrifices for the other eight cars who almost got flooded but didn't because their cars alerted them. By the time they got out of the car, they had the same mindset. My spirit was so grateful, and their gratefulness just made the rescue worthwhile. I know and feel that I am no hero: God planned for me to be there at that appointed time, and I simply obeyed Him.

I know that I am exactly where I am supposed to be, but I have recently been having a very hard time adjusting to the adult world. I am in desperate need of like-minded friends in my area or a mentor. This process is new, lonely, and uncomfortable. Because of loneliness, I settled for a guy who did not see my worth and I allowed my confidence to be affected terribly. I also backslid. Then, my boss started living up to his reputation, and his actions affected me as well. Only negativity was being poured into me for months. It took me a while to remember that I was the apple of God's eye, a royal priesthood, and a queen.

My confidence was so low that I almost decided not to publish this book. Before it was published, it had been completed for three months, but the enemy tried to play me and tell me that it would not be a blessing to others. I did not have to go down that road, but I chose to be impatient about trusting God for good company. I ultimately got what I deserved. Trust me: it is so much easier to wait and trust God. BUT…I'M BACKKKK. I am finally at peace again after battling with that situation. I have been working on myself, for myself, by myself. I refused to allow ANYONE to ever have that much power over me ever again.

All of my experiences, distant and recent, have led me here: my vision is to not only counsel people in my private practice, but to reach people all over the world. I want to make my voice heard for those who were silenced by their situations. I am going to make sure that the sequel to this book is LIT! My name will be remembered and God will continue to get all of the glory.

I wrote this book to encourage you all, and to let you know that the good, bad, and the ugly HAD to happen in order to mold you into the person you are today. I am thankful for it all because I blossomed through the concrete when there was not a crack in sight. I encourage everyone who took the time to read my story to declare a forecast of 100% winning every day, in spite of how the weather looks outside.

Even when you meet someone whose forecast is nothing but thunderstorms, grab an umbrella and refuse to allow them to rain on your parade. Wear rain boots so that you can stomp through the puddles too. Often we feel as if God has forgotten about us when He is really sharpening us. What happens in life may not feel good TO us, but it is good FOR us in the long run. When you have faith, you will start to look for a lesson in every situation. Although I am still trying to figure out what my purpose is, I know a part of it is speaking life into others.

As I mentioned before, I help myself when I help others. I am aware that my inner light shines, and it attracts people to me who need a positive outlook on life. I am a living sacrifice, and I ask God for the "Godfidence" that allows me to pour into His people. Be encouraged and know God's purpose will always trump your plans. Simply ask for His will to be done and trust the process. Let's please share our testimony with others because *we overcome by the blood of the lamb and by the words of our testimonies* (Revelation 12:11). Let's all overcome together.

ABOUT THE AUTHOR

KIERRA ALEXIS CARTER

Kierra Alexis Carter was born in Florence, South Carolina on August 25, 1995. Her parents are Anita Hines and Kenneth Carter. Kierra has two older brothers; Kenneth and Kaleb. Kierra enjoys singing, dancing, acting, modeling, motivational speaking, traveling, and eating. Kierra Alexis Carter is an alumnus of Wilson High School and Claflin University. She is also a current student at South Carolina State University. Kierra Carter made her journey at Claflin worthwhile. She was Miss Freshman, Miss Student Support Services, a cheerleader for three years (co-captain), and the chaplain of Corson Hall.

During her sophomore year, she became a member of the Alice Carson Tisdale Honors College, Miss Kleist Hall, a member of Friends of the Earth, the first African American Miss Florence 2015, and a Miss South Carolina Pageant participant. She is also the founder of Helping Everyone Avoid Loneliness, which is a support group for college students who are facing internal obstacles in school. During her junior year, she became a member of Psi Chi International Honor Society; Golden Key International Honour Society; National Honor Society of Leadership and Success; and vice president of the Psychology Club.

Finally, during her senior year, she became a member of Alpha Kappa Alpha Sorority, Incorporated and served as Miss Claflin University 2016-2017. Upon many other accolades, Kierra graduated Summa Cum Laude with a Bachelor of Arts Degree in Psychology with a double minor in Mass Communications and Theatre. She recently recorded two commercials for BET, was honored with a Girls Rock

Award from Palmetto Youth Academy and was honored at New Ebenezer Baptist Church for her community service. She is a state employee in South Carolina with plans of becoming a Counselor with a private practice and a motivational speaker.

Made in the USA
Columbia, SC
31 May 2021

38336636R00064